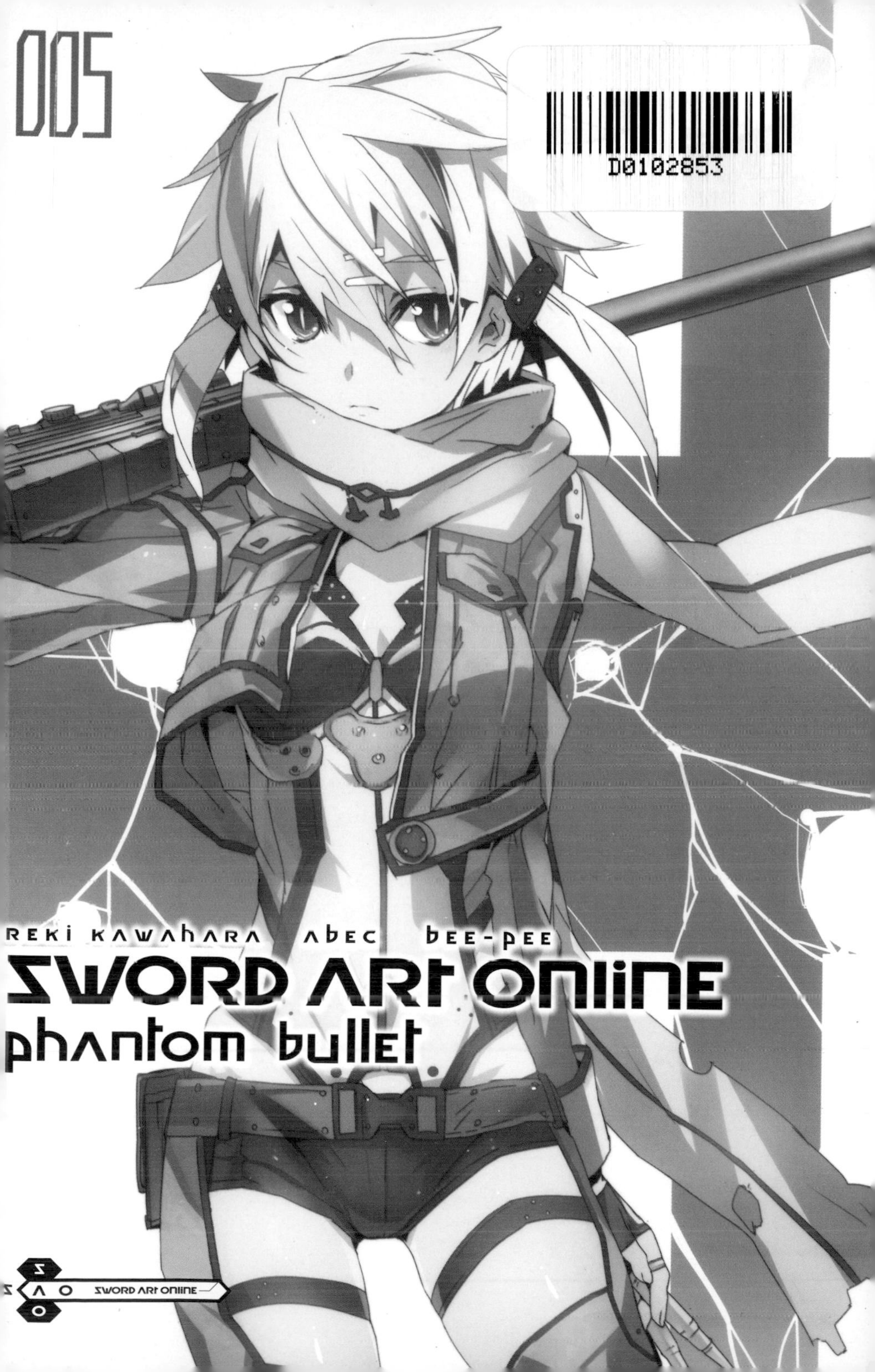

REKI KAWAHARA abec bee-pee

SWORD ART ONLINE

phantom bullet

"Ice. I am a machine of coldest ice."

Sinon § A player in *Gun Gale Online*, an MMO of guns and steel. She dispatches her foes with the massive Hecate II sniper rifle.

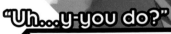

"Uh...y-you do?"

Kazuto Kirigaya § The Black Swordsman, who successfully beat *SAO*, the nightmare MMO. Goes by Kirito.

"I think I understand why you brought me here."

Asuna Yuuki § Kazuto's girlfriend, who once was Kirito's partner back in *SAO*.

"I heard about your big battle the other day. Seems you were quite the hero."

Kyouji Shinkawa § Shino's former classmate. After their first conversation in the library, he recommends that Shino start playing *GGO* with him.

"...It's not true. We lost four out of our six squadron members. Given that we were the ones waiting in ambush, that's hardly what you'd call a victory."

Shino Asada § A girl living alone in the big city and attending her first year of high school. She plays *GGO* to escape the trauma of her past.

"…This is the true power, the true strength! Carve this name and the terror it commands into your hearts, you fools! My name, and the name of my weapon, is….*Death Gun*!!"

Death Gun § A mysterious avatar who commits PK (player-killing) in *GGO*. Players shot by Death Gun in *GGO* also die in real life.

Abbreviated to *GGO*. In a world ruled by firearms and steel, players strive to be the greatest gunner of them all. PK-ing is encouraged, and the game system rewards defeating other players in the same way it does defeating AI-controlled monsters. The weapons of *GGO* are classified as either live-ammo or optical guns, and the currently held theory is that live-ammo guns are best against players while optics are best against monsters. There are major differences between the two aside from their stats—optical guns all have fictional names and hand-designed appearances, while the live-ammo guns are modeled and named after actual existing guns. For this reason, the majority of *GGO* players are gun fanatics.

PGM ULTIMA RATIO HECATE II

This gun is 138 centimeters (4.5 feet) long, weighing 13.8 kilograms (30.4 pounds). It fires enormous .50-caliber rounds (12.7 by 99 millimeters, or 0.5 inches wide). In the real world, this would be categorized as an anti-materiel sniper rifle meant for piercing military vehicles or structures—its overwhelming power makes it forbidden to use against human targets. The name "Hecate" was taken from the Greek goddess of the underworld.

The Hecate II within the world of *GGO* is an anti-materiel sniper rifle, of which there are only ten on the entire server. It is one of the rarest of the excavated weapons, which are not available for purchase in shops. It trades at the very high price of 20 million credits, which is about 200,000 yen in real money.

SWORD ART ONLINE phantom bullet

VOLUME 5

Reki Kawahara

abec

bee-pee

YEN ON

NEW YORK

SWORD ART ONLINE 5: Phantom Bullet
REKI KAWAHARA

Translation by Stephen Paul

SWORD ART ONLINE
© REKI KAWAHARA 2010
All rights reserved.
First published in Japan in 2010 by
KADOKAWA CORPORATION, Tokyo.
English translation rights arranged with
KADOKAWA CORPORATION, Tokyo,
through Tuttle-Mori Agency, Inc., Tokyo.

English translation © 2015 Yen Press, LLC

Yen On
1290 Avenue of the Americas
New York, NY 10104
www.yenpress.com

Yen On is an imprint of Yen Press, LLC.
The Yen On name and logo are trademarks of Yen Press, LLC.

First Yen On edition: August 2015

ISBN: 978-0-316-29644-1

10 9 8 7 6 5 4

LSC-C

Printed in the United States of America

"THIS MIGHT BE A GAME, BUT IT'S NOT SOMETHING YOU PLAY."

—Akihiko Kayaba, *Sword Art Online* programmer

SWORD ART Online
phantom bullet

Reki Kawahara

aboc

bee-pee

"I'm telling you, the theory that AGI is the One True Stat is total nonsense," screeched a high-pitched male voice, echoing off the walls of the spacious pub. "Sure, Agility's an important stat. Having an extremely high firing speed and evasion were enough to make you one of the best—until now."

The owner of the cocky voice was a player in a four-sided holo-panel, floating high in the middle of the dimly lit establishment.

The panel was playing a popular program called *This Week's Winners* on the Net channel MMO Stream. You could watch their videos on real TVs or computers, but given that they also streamed into the inns and pubs of countless VRMMO worlds, most players preferred to watch it in-game.

Especially when the segment's guest happened to be from their world.

"But that's all in the past now. I've got one simple message for all my friends who wasted their lives raising AGI for the past eight months: Rest in peace."

His obnoxious taunt was met with boos and jeers from the large pub, and a few glass bottles and mugs flew across the room, smashing against the wall into little polygonal shards.

But one man did not join the raucous shouting. He waited on the sofa in the back, curled up into a ball. He eyed the rest of the pub with a cold stare from between the low ghillie suit hood and the thick cloth that covered the lower half of his face.

The gloating man on the program was bad enough, but the slack-faced idiots gazing at the holo-TV were even worse. They all booed and shouted, but it was almost more of a game to them than a serious protest.

He couldn't understand what made them act so empty-headed. The man on the program had seized the mantle of the game's best player through sheer coincidence and was now its greatest exploiter as well. He was taking a share of the subscription fee that every player in the game paid, reveling in his pro gamer status.

Everyone must have felt the same jealousy and hatred of the gloating champion. If that dark emotion was ugly, then hiding it and pretending to laugh it off was both ugly *and* farcical.

The man felt his entire body tense beneath the suit. A breath hissed between his clenched teeth. It wasn't time yet. He would pull the trigger a little later.

Back on the holo-panel, the camera zoomed out to show the program's host sitting to the right of the champion, as well as another guest on his left.

The host, a girl dressed in technopop fashion, bubbled, "Those are some pretty powerful words, but I guess I should expect that from the top player in *Gun Gale Online*, the most hardcore of all the VRMMOs."

"Well, I figured I'd only get one chance to be on MMO Stream, so I gotta say my piece while I can."

"Oh, but you'll be competing in the next Bullet of Bullets, won't you?"

"Of course. And I'm in it to win it," he declared directly at the camera, brushing back his long, blue-silver hair. The pub erupted in boos again.

MMO Stream was not produced exclusively for *Gun Gale Online* (GGO), but the guests and host were all in avatar form. *This Week's Winners* was an interview program that hosted the best players from various virtual reality massive multiplayer games, and the current guests were the champion and runner-up of the Bullet of Bullets, the battle-royale tournament held last month in *GGO*.

"The thing is, Zexceed," the runner-up interrupted, clearly tired of hearing the silver-haired man preen, "isn't BoB all about solo encounters? There's no guarantee you'll have the same results a second time, so it's rather silly to act like this victory was guaranteed by your player's build, if you ask me."

"No way. This result was a manifestation of a general trend in *GGO*. I realize that you don't want to admit this, Yamikaze, as you're playing an agility build," the champion Zexceed retorted. "It's true that until now, pumping up your AGI so you could rapid-fire live-ammo weapons was the prevailing style. You'd earn a bonus to evasion that way, too, which helps make up for the weak durability rating. But unlike a single-player game, the balance of an MMO changes over time. When you're dealing with level-based systems, you can't rearrange your stats freely, so you have to allocate those points with an eye toward the future. The best style in one level zone might not be the best in the next. You understand that, right? The guns we'll see next will have higher and higher strength and accuracy requirements to equip. This idea that you can just dodge out of harm's way in every encounter is going the way of the dodo. The battle between me and Yamikaze was that process in a microcosm. Most of your gun's power was neutralized by my bulletproof armor, and yet 70 percent of my shots landed. I'll say it right now: We're entering the age of the STR-VIT build."

The man named Yamikaze grimaced with displeasure.

"But…that's only because you succeeded in getting a rare gun whose strength requirement was just within your grasp, right before the tournament started. How much did you pay for that?"

"Nuh-uh, that was a drop, fair and square. But if you want to put it that way, the greatest stat of all is your real-life luck. Ha-ha-ha!"

The man on the sofa moved his right hand, staring at the laughing, silver-haired Zexceed on the holo-panel with utter loathing. He found the grip sticking out of his waist holster and squeezed the cool metal. Very soon. It would happen very soon. He checked the time readout in the corner of his vision. One minute, twenty seconds.

At the table nearest to him, two players nursed their mugs and muttered to themselves.

"*Keh!* Listen to him prattle on. Who do you think started the whole AGI build movement in the first place? It was Zexceed!"

"Now it looks like that was all a trap to draw the player population down the wrong direction…And we fell for it, hook, line, and sinker…"

"Think that means his new Strength and Vitality fad is another bluff?"

"Makes you wonder what'll come next. Boosting Luck?"

"You should try it."

"Hell no."

They both cackled. The sound only made the man's anger hotter. How could they laugh like that, knowing they'd been fooled? It made no sense.

But those stupid chuckles will freeze on their tongues very soon. Once they see true power—who the real champion is.

It was time.

He stood without a sound. He strode between the tables, step after step. No one paid him any attention.

"Fools…You will know terror," he muttered, and came to a stop directly beneath the holo-panel in the center of the pub. He pulled a crude handgun from the holster on the waist of his ghillie suit.

It gleamed black and metallic, like pure, compressed darkness. Even the grip was metal, and in the center of the vertical serrations on the handle was a star-shaped brand. By any standard, it looked like any old automatic pistol, nothing special.

But this gun had *true power.*

He clicked the slide back, loading a fresh round, then slowly, easily held the gun directly upward at the huge holo-panel. Right at the forehead of the cocky, laughing Zexceed.

He held the gun in place for a few moments, until uneasy murmuring broke out around him. Although PKing was essentially unlimited in *GGO*, the exception was in town, where attacking others was impossible. He could fire the gun, but not only would it not harm any players, it wouldn't even affect the environment.

His pointless display caused a few stifled giggles to arise around him, but he kept the black gun trained perfectly still, using an isosceles stance. In the midst of the holo-panel, Zexceed was still taunting.

Somewhere in the real world, Zexceed's actual body was lying down, wearing an AmuSphere on his head, while he was logged in to the MMO Stream virtual studio. Naturally, he would have no way of knowing that there was a player pointing a gun at his image on TV in a certain pub in the business quarter of SBC Glocken, capital city of the world of *Gun Gale Online*.

Despite this, the man opened his mouth and shouted for all to hear.

"Zexceed! False victor! Taste the judgment of true power!!"

With the shocked stares of the entire room upon him, he raised his left arm, tracing a cross with his fingertips from forehead to chest, then left shoulder to right.

As he lowered his left hand, he pulled the trigger with his right. The slide blew back, producing the yellow flash of gunfire. There was a sharp, dry pop.

Beneath the dim lights of the pub, the metal bullet flew directly into the holo-panel and created brief little splintering effects.

That was it. Zexceed was still glibly chattering away on the program.

Actual laughter broke out now. Some of the crowd groaned and muttered about how embarrassing the whole display was. Meanwhile, Zexceed's voice was audible above the murmurs.

"—don't you see, even if you include stats and skill selection, the ultimate factor is the player's ski—"

He stopped midsentence. The pub focused on the holo-panel again.

Zexceed was frozen in place, his eyes wide and mouth open. His hand slowly, slowly rose to clutch at his chest.

The next moment, he disappeared, leaving only a 3D-modeled chair behind. The host quickly spoke up.

"Uh-oh, looks like he lost connection. Don't change that channel, folks, I'm sure he'll be right back with us..."

But no one in the pub heard her. In dead silence, they were all looking at the man again.

He lowered the gun and held it vertically, then slowly turned, his eyes lingering upon the various denizens of the room. Once he had completed a full rotation, the man held the black gun high and shouted again.

"...This is the true power, the true strength! Carve this name and the terror it commands into your hearts, you fools!"

He sucked in a deep breath.

"My name, and the name of my weapon, is...*Death Gun!!*"

He returned the firearm to his holster and swiped the menu open with his left hand.

As he hit the log-out button, he felt a tremendous sense of triumph, and with it, an even stronger, burning hunger.

1

"Welcome. Party of one?"

The waiter bowed graciously. I told him I was waiting for some-one, and then looked around the spacious café. A loud, carefree voice broke the calm, from a table near a window in the back.

"Hey, Kirito, over here!"

The hushed, refined chatter that had flowed atop the classical background music fell silent, replaced by disapproving stares. I hunched my shoulders and rushed over to the source of the shout. With my faded leather flight jacket and distressed jeans, I was firmly out of place next to the middle-aged, manicured women of wealth on their shopping trips, who filled the room. Their irritation at the party responsible for summoning me here was growing by the moment.

If my partner had been a lovely young lady, that would be one thing, but it was a man in a suit who waved me over. I plopped into the seat across from him, not bothering to hide my dissatisfaction.

The waiter instantly swooped in and offered me a glass of water and a fresh hand towel, along with a menu. I grabbed it, noting the leather finish, and the fellow across the table piped up.

"This is on me, so order whatever you like."

"I figured as much," I replied as I looked over the menu, only to discover the cheapest item on it was the chou à la crème at

1,200 yen. I quickly made to order a simple cup of coffee, but it occurred to me that this man was a highly paid official and would just expense the meal, putting it on the taxpayers' tab. Feeling like an idiot, I ordered a string of items, trying to act natural.

"Erm...I'll have the parfait au chocolat...the mille-feuille framboise...and a hazelnut coffee," I said, somehow managing to avoid tripping over my tongue. The total came out to 3,900 yen. I almost felt like finishing with a hamburger and a shake and demanding the change. Incidentally, those items were chosen randomly off the menu, and I had no idea what I was actually getting.

"They'll be right up."

The waiter departed smoothly and I looked up with a sigh.

The man across the table chowing down on a giant serving of pudding piled high with cream was Seijirou Kikuoka. He featured thick black-rimmed glasses, an utterly plain haircut, and narrow, fussy features that brought a Japanese language teacher to mind—but despite all of this, he was actually an ambitious fast riser within the government. He worked for the Ministry of Internal Affairs' Telecommunications Bureau, Advanced Network Division, Second Office: known within the ministry as the Virtual Network Management Division, aka "Virtual Division."

In other words, this man was a government agent—or scapegoat—in charge of monitoring the chaotic and lawless VR world. He often lamented that he'd been sequestered in this position, and I believed that was probably the case.

Misfortunate Mr. Kikuoka carried the last blissful bite of pudding to his mouth and looked up with a mischievous grin.

"Hi there, Kirito. Sorry for forcing you to make the trip out here."

"If you were really sorry, you wouldn't ask me to come to Ginza."

I wiped my hands with the faintly citrus-smelling hand towel, then added, "Plus, I don't know why you think you should call me Kirito."

"Oh, don't be mean. Wasn't I the first person who rushed to your bedside when you woke up in the hospital a year ago?"

Sadly, that was true. The very first person to visit me after my awakening from that game of death was Kikuoka, who'd been a government agent working for the task force on that case.

At the time, I used polite speech with him, but as time went on and I realized that he was not contacting me solely out of altruistic concern, I gradually got more snarky and sarcastic. Or perhaps he was manipulating me into that attitude—but I was probably overthinking it.

I glanced at Kikuoka, who seemed to be seriously considering another order for himself, and warned myself not to let him manipulate me.

"I heard they found some huge rare-earth deposit in Sagami Bay, and all the senior officials from the appropriate ministries were dancing a jig to 'Turkey in the Straw.' Yet here you are, wondering if you should pony up for another cream puff," I jabbed.

Kikuoka looked up, blinked several times, then beamed.

"Doesn't matter, because none of the profit they make excavating that will go to the Ministry of Internal Affairs. I think I'll hold off, for the benefit of the national budget."

He snapped the menu shut and I gave him another sigh.

"Can we get to the business at hand, then? I can already guess what it is: another virtual crime needing hands-on research?"

"I love how quick you are on the uptake, Kirito," Kikuoka replied without missing a step. He pulled out a super-thin tablet computer from the briefcase on the seat next to him.

That's right—he's using me, a survivor of the Sword Art Online *Incident, the worst online crime in Japan's history, as a provider of information.*

According to what I'd read, the regular police called their informants "cooperators" or "monitors," and the act of periodically handing out rewards in exchange for information was called "managing contacts." If that was the case, you could say that that Kikuoka was "managing" me with the occasional piece of cake.

That wasn't exactly a good feeling, but I owed him for breaking the rules and telling me which hospital Asuna was being kept in. If I hadn't had that info, I wouldn't have been able to find Asuna Yuuki so quickly again in the real world. That meant I wouldn't have learned about Nobuyuki Sugou's diabolical scheme, nor would I have been able to prevent him from taking Asuna as his own.

So for the time being, I was content to be Kikuoka's monitor. I just wasn't going to bother kissing his ass, or holding back from ordering the most expensive cake on the menu.

Meanwhile, my benevolent manager, totally unaware of what was running through my head, traced a finger along the tablet and slowly muttered, "See, the thing is, the number of virtual-space crimes are on the rise again..."

"Oh? Break it down for me."

"Well...we've got over a hundred claims of virtual asset theft or damage just for November alone. On top of that, thirteen cases of real-life assault stemming from trouble within VR games. One of which led to death...You've probably already heard about that one, since it was all over the media—the one with the replica Western-style sword that was honed to an edge, then swung around at Shinjuku Station, killing two. Four feet long and eight pounds, yikes! I don't know how you swing something like that around."

"Apparently he was hallucinating because of the drugs he took to keep him going through all those play sessions. It sounds horrifying when you look at that one case, but while I don't want to minimize it, if that's all there is, compared to the big picture..."

"Yes, exactly. It's just a tiny fraction of the total number of assault cases nationwide, and it would be silly to suggest a short-sighted conclusion, like VRMMOs are brewing social unrest. But I remember what you said earlier..."

"That VRMMO games lower the mental barriers to causing others physical harm in the real world. Yes, I'll admit that," I said. The waiter appeared without a sound and placed two plates and a cup in front of me.

"Will that be all for today?"

I nodded, and he placed the receipt on the corner of the table facedown, so as not to display the shocking total price. I took a sip of the nutty, fragrant coffee and continued.

"PKing is becoming more and more customary in certain games, and you could see that as a training exercise for real murder. The ones who are really pushing the boundaries even have realistic blood spray for severed veins, and guts that spill out of your stomach. The people who get really obsessed with those even commit suicide as a means of logging out."

I heard a cough, and looked over my shoulder to see two high-class ladies glaring at me, aghast. I ducked my head and lowered my voice.

"It's not hard to imagine someone who does that every day in their spare time deciding to try it out in real life. I agree that some kind of measures need to be taken. But outlawing it won't work."

"No go?"

"No go."

I carefully scooped up some of the many-layered cake of fine sponge and pink cream with the golden spoon, and lifted it to my mouth. It occurred to me that a single spoonful of this dessert probably cost a hundred yen. The cake practically melted on my tongue.

"You'd have to completely isolate them on the Net. In terms of the actual bandwidth consumed, VRMMOs are actually fairly lightweight. If you try to crack down domestically, the users and developers will just go overseas."

"Hmm..."

Kikuoka looked down at the table, silent for several seconds.

"...That mille-feuille looks really good. Can I have a bite?"

"..."

I sighed for the third time and pushed the plate over to him. The dignified government employee gleefully tore off about 280 yen of cake and shoved it into his mouth.

"Well, here's what I wonder, Kirito...Why do they want to kill each other, rather than get along? Seems like that would be more fun."

"...You've played a bit of *ALfheim Online*, so you should understand. Even in the days before full-dive technology came along, MMORPGs have always been about competition. When you have an online game with no set end point, what keeps the players motivated? When you get down to it...they want that instinctual feeling of superiority, of being the best."

"Oh?"

He raised an eyebrow as he chewed, seeking elaboration. I wondered why I had to explain all of this, then vindictively decided to give him what he wanted.

"It's not just about video games. Isn't the desire to be praised and be better than others the cornerstone of our society? You must know that from personal experience. You see other bureaucrats in the ministry who came from better schools, and you're jealous of their more rapid career success. Meanwhile, it feels good to mingle with those not on the career fast track, and see how much better you have it. You can only stuff yourself with that cake because you've found an equilibrium between superiority and inferiority."

Kikuoka swallowed the mille-feuille and smiled awkwardly.

"Wow, you don't hold back, do you? What about you, Kirito? Have you gotten that equilibrium?"

"..."

I had a mountain of an inferiority complex, but I wasn't going to admit that to him. Instead, I kept a straight face.

"...Well, I do have a girlfriend."

"And in that one sense, I am exceedingly jealous of you, Kirito.

Mind introducing me to a girl in *ALO* sometime? I wouldn't mind getting to know that sylph leader."

"Just to warn you, if you try to hit on her by saying you're a high-ranking bureaucrat, she'll cut you in two."

"At her hands, I wouldn't mind. So?"

"So, it's extremely difficult to gain that kind of superiority in the real world. It's the kind of thing that doesn't come without a ton of work. Work to get good grades, work to get better at sports, work to be handsome, or pretty...They all take an incredible amount of time and energy, and they don't guarantee you any success."

"I see. Like how I nearly studied myself to death for college entrance exams, and I didn't get into Tokyo University," he said, grinning for some reason. I decided not to crack on him, and got straight to the point instead.

"But in a massive multiplayer online role-playing game, if you spend your time there at the expense of real life, you're guaranteed to get stronger. You'll get rare loot. Sure, it takes effort, but it's all a game. It's way more fun than studying or lifting weights. When you walk down the main street of town in your expensive gear and that high-level indicator next to your name, you can feel the jealous stares of the characters weaker than you... or at least, you feel like you do. If you go out to hunt monsters, you can destroy them in one hit with your overwhelming power and save parties in need. Then they thank you and look up to you—"

"Or at least, it feels that way?"

"...It's a one-dimensional view, I admit. There are other facets to MMOs. There have been online games for the purpose of communication above all else for years and years, but they've never been a hit the way MMORPGs have."

"I see what you're saying. Because you don't feel the satisfaction of superiority in those games?"

"Exactly. Then VRMMOs came along. Now you can actually

feel those stares as you walk down the street. You don't have to imagine them coming through the monitor."

"Uh-huh. I've seen the jealous looks that you and Asuna get when you stroll through Ygg City."

"...Wow, you don't hold back, do you? At any rate, anyone playing a VRMMO can enjoy that superiority if they sink the time into it. And it's a kind of superiority that's simpler, more primitive, and more instinctual than what you get for good grades, or being good at soccer."

"Meaning...?"

"Meaning *strength*. Physical, muscular strength. The power to destroy your opponent with your own hands. It's like a drug."

"...Strength...The greatest power of all," Kikuoka murmured nostalgically. "Every boy dreams of having that kind of strength someday...You read a fighting manga, then imagine going through the same training. But once you realize it doesn't come that easy, you switch dreams to something that's a little more realistic...You're saying that in the VRMMO world, you can experience that dream again?"

I nodded and, after my lengthy speech, quenched my dry throat with a sip of coffee.

"That's right. One of the heavy martial arts simulation games is so focused on reality, they formed partnerships with actual martial arts schools."

"Oh? Meaning?"

"Meaning that if you raise your in-game character to a certain level, you can actually be a registered expert in Whatchamacallit Karate, or So-and-So Kung Fu. They set the game in a realistically modeled Shinjuku and Shibuya, and you get to dole out justice to a bunch of unruly thugs. The problem is, it doesn't teach you the proper mind-set of a martial artist. So anyone who gets completely sucked into that kind of game only goes through the motions, if you will...and sadly, I can't deny the possibility that some of them will be curious to try out the moves they learned in the real world."

"I see...So you're worried about the presence of strength in a VRMMO bleeding over into reality. Say, Kirito," Kikuoka said, looking directly into my eyes, "do you really think that's just a mental thing?"

"...What do you mean?"

"Do you think it's not just lowering the mental hurdles to violence and teaching the player the knowledge and skill to fight... but that it could also be having some kind of physical effect on the bodies of the players?"

Now it was my turn to stop and think it over.

"Are you asking if that guy swinging an eight-pound sword in Shinjuku might have earned his arm strength through a game somehow?"

"Yes, exactly."

"Hmm...Well, I hear that they've only just begun studying the long-term effect of the full-dive system on human nerves. I mean, your actual body's just lying down, so your core strength would obviously fall, but maybe there's some effect on our ability to tap that subconscious panic strength...Wouldn't you know that better than me, though?"

"I did an interview with what they call a cerebro-physiologist, but I didn't understand a word of it. Now, I know it was a very roundabout way to get to the point, but this is what I wanted to talk to you about. Look at this."

Kikuoka tapped at the tablet and showed it to me. I examined the screen and saw a head shot of an unfamiliar man along with a profile containing an address and other details. He had long, unkempt hair, silver-rimmed glasses, and heavy fat around his cheeks and neck.

"...Who's this?"

Kikuoka took the tablet back and traced it with his fingers.

"Let's see, it was last month...November fourteenth. At an apartment building in the Nakano Ward of Tokyo, the landlord was cleaning and noticed a funny smell. He narrowed it down to one unit, but there was no response to the intercom or the phone. Yet the lights were on in the apartment. So he undid the electronic lock and entered the apartment to find…Tamotsu Shigemura, age twenty-six, dead. They determined he was dead for five and a half days. The room was cluttered, but not ransacked, and the body was lying on the bed. Around his head was…"

"An AmuSphere," I finished, envisioning the full-dive headgear unit made of two metal rings, one of which was in my own room. Kikuoka nodded.

"That's right. They contacted the family at once, and had an autopsy performed. The cause of death was sudden cardiac arrest."

"Cardiac arrest? Meaning that his heart just stopped working? Why did it stop?"

"We don't know."

"…"

"Too much time passed after his death, and the likelihood of criminal involvement was low, so they didn't bother with a detailed autopsy. The one thing we know is that he hadn't eaten anything in about two days, and was still logged in."

I furrowed my brow again. It wasn't all that rare to hear stories like this. Eating "food" in the virtual world caused a false sense of fulfillment that lasted several hours, even if the user hadn't eaten anything in the real world. The ultra-hardcore gamers found that this cut down on food costs and gave them more time to play, so it wasn't rare to hear about players who only ate one meal every two days.

Naturally, if that pattern continued, there would be ill effects on the body. Malnutrition was an obvious outcome, and if you had a seizure while living alone, unable to care for yourself…the natural outcome was much like this case. It happened from time to time.

I closed my eyes for a moment and said a silent prayer for Shigemura, then opened my mouth.

"It is very sad, but…"

"Exactly. It's sad, but common nowadays. This kind of death isn't news anymore, and it's hard to get a tally because families don't want people to know about them dying while in a game. In a way, this is also a case of VRMMOs contributing to the death numbers…"

"But you didn't bring me out here just to talk about ordinary cases, did you? What really happened here?"

Kikuoka took another glance at the tablet before answering.

"There was only one VR game installed on Shigemura's AmuSphere—*Gun Gale Online*. Have you heard of it?"

"Well, of course. It's the only MMO in Japan that has pro players. I've never tried it myself."

"He was apparently the very top player in *Gun Gale Online*, which they abbreviate to *GGO*. He won a tournament they held to determine the very best back in October. Player name: Zexceed."

"So…was he logged in to *GGO* when he died?"

"Actually, he wasn't. He was in character as Zexceed while appearing on the MMO Stream online channel."

"Oh…on *This Week's Winners*, then. Now that you mention it, I seem to recall a story about a time they had to cancel an episode because the guest dropped out partway…"

"That's probably the one. He had the heart attack in the middle of the program. We know the time down to the second, thanks to the recorded log. Now, as far as what we haven't been able to confirm yet, there's a very strange blog post someone put up about an event that happened in *GGO* right at the same time."

"Strange?"

"You know how MMO Stream plays even within the world of *GGO*?"

"Yeah, they air it in pubs and places like that."

"Well, it was being streamed in a bar within SBC Glocken, the capital city in the world of *GGO*. And at exactly the time in question, they reported that a player was acting very strangely."

"…"

"Seems he fired his gun at the image of Zexceed on the TV, shouting about judgment and that he needed to die and so on. One of the other players at the scene just happened to be in the process of a sound recording, and he uploaded it to a video site. The file had a Japan Standard Time readout on it, and according to that, he fired at the TV at precisely...eleven thirty PM and two seconds, November ninth. And Shigemura suddenly disappeared from the program at eleven thirty and fifteen seconds."

"...Gotta be a coincidence," I said, pulling the other plate in front of me.

I split the brown, circular object with my spoon and took a bite. The chill of the dessert caught me by surprise; I'd thought it was a cake, but it was some kind of ice cream. My mouth was filled with a rich chocolate flavor with only the barest level of sweetness, the bitterness only amplifying the unpleasant nature of Kikuoka's story.

Once I'd tucked away about a third of the dish, I continued.

"The jealousy and hate the best player in *GGO* gets has to be far and away worse than any other MMO. It would take some guts to fire a gun at him directly, but it doesn't seem that crazy that someone would shoot a TV."

"Right, but there's another one."

"...What?"

The spoon stopped halfway to my mouth. Kikuoka still wore his excellent poker face.

"This one happened about ten days ago, on November twenty-eighth. Another body found in a two-floor apartment building, this time in Omiya Ward of the city of Saitama. A door-to-door newspaper salesman got angry that there was no response despite the lights being on, and thought the resident was ignoring him, so he turned the knob and found that it was unlocked. Inside he saw another person on their bed, AmuSphere in place, with a decomposing smell..."

A very intentional cough interrupted our conversation, and

Kikuoka and I looked over to see the same two ladies staring at us with the power of floating beholders. Kikuoka had nerves of steel, though, and gave them a slight bow before continuing his story.

"...Putting aside the state of the body, it was once again determined to be heart failure. This one was...well, the name doesn't matter. Male, age thirty-one. Another influential player in *GGO*. His character name was...Usujio Tarako? 'Lightly Salted Cod Roe'? Is that right?"

"There was a guy in *SAO* named Hokkai Ikura, meaning 'North Sea Salmon Roe,' so maybe he was a relative. And was this Tarako on TV as well?"

"No, this one was actually in the game. Based on the Amu-Sphere's log, the signal died about three days before the body was found, at exactly ten o'clock and four seconds PM, November twenty-fifth. That about lines up with the estimated time of death. At the time he was at a meeting with his squadron—that's what they call guilds, apparently—in the central square of Glocken. As he was delivering a fiery speech on the pulpit, a player invaded the meeting and shot at him. You don't take damage in town, from what I understand, but when he turned to yell at the intruder, he just dropped offline. Of course, this information comes from a message board, so it's hard to get an accurate picture..."

"Was the player who came up firing the same one as with Zexceed?"

"I think we can assume so. Said something about judgment and power, and dropped the same name as the previous time."

"...Which was?"

Kikuoka looked at the tablet and squinted.

"Looks like...Death Gun."

"Death...Gun..."

I put the spoon down on the empty plate and let the name echo inside my head. A character's name, no matter how goofy it might sound, was a huge part of the first impression you gave to others. The name Death Gun suggested the coldness of black metal to me.

"And you're certain that it was cardiac arrest that both Zexceed and Usujio Tarako died of?"

"Meaning?"

"There wasn't any...damage to their brains?"

The instant I said it, Kikuoka grinned in understanding.

"I wondered about that myself, and I asked the doctors who performed the autopsies, but they didn't find any bleeding or blockage in the brain that suggested any kind of abnormality."

"..."

"Besides, with the NerveGear—er, do you mind if I bring that up?"

"It's fine."

"With the NerveGear, when it killed its user, it sent a flash of microwave power that was so powerful it burned out the emitters and destroyed a part of the brain. But the AmuSphere was built so that it couldn't emit waves that strong. The developers swear that it only sends exceedingly low-level information signals to the sensory center of the brain."

"So you've even checked with the manufacturer. Quite a lot of legwork you've put into a conclusion provided by coincidence and rumors, isn't it, Mr. Kikuoka?"

I stared at the narrow eyes beyond the glasses. For an instant, his face went blank, then he chuckled.

"Being stuck in a dead-end position leaves you with plenty of time on your hands."

"You should help us advance the front line in Aincrad sometime, then. Eugene says you've got a lot of talent as a mage."

As a matter of fact, I didn't take this man for the bumbling paper pusher he appeared to be. The reason he'd made his own character in *ALO* was not out of interest in playing the game, but as a means of gathering information and experience on the virtual world for the sake of his job. The business card he gave me on our first meeting said Ministry of Internal Affairs, sure enough, but even that was suspicious to me. He seemed like he could belong to some other department—more secret, aligned with national safety.

But regardless of that, back when the Virtual Division was still the *SAO* Incident Rescue Task Force, it was through his efforts that the government was able to enact a system to hospitalize all the players afflicted. Because of that, and his help with Asuna, I usually treated him with 60 percent respect and 40 percent suspicion.

Kikuoka scratched the back of his head and smiled shyly.

"Memorizing those spell words isn't the hard part—it's actually saying them. I've never been good with tongue twisters. But at any rate, I think this whole thing is 90 percent coincidence or hearsay, like you. So this is all just theoretical. Kirito, do you think it's possible? Could someone stop another player's heart by shooting them in the game?"

His words caused a scene to play out inside my head. I frowned.

A shooter…dressed in black, face unseen, pulling the trigger while pointing into empty space. A black, illusionary bullet leaving the barrel, tearing through the virtual wall and into the actual network, as packets of information fly in every direction. From router to router, server to server, the bullet makes hard right angles and charges on its way. Eventually it reaches an apartment, where it emerges from the LAN router on the wall as a real bullet, and into the heart of the man lying on the bed…

I shook my head to clear the image and raised a finger.

"I don't think it's completely impossible…but let's say this Death Gun fellow was able to send some kind of signal to the AmuSpheres of Zexceed and Usujio Tarako…"

"Well, let's start with that. Is it even possible?"

"Hmm…First of all, it would have to be just a normal signal, not some kind of mysterious, fatality-causing power. Do you remember the panic around the Imagenerator virus?"

Imagenerator was a privately developed mail program from the AmuSphere. The user dove into a virtual space generated by the software and delivered a message into a camera, which the program compressed into a mailable format. When the other party accepted the e-mail, the sender's virtual body appeared before them to speak the message. As new features like video, sound, and even texture were added, the program turned into a huge hit.

But soon security holes in the program were discovered, and virus mails began to take advantage of them. The moment the mail arrived, if the user was already middive, the program started a forced preview, startling the user with shocking images and sound, usually something sexual and/or grotesque.

They patched it immediately and prevented further damage, naturally, but…

"Nearly every person with an AmuSphere has installed Imagenerator by now. If there was some undiscovered back door, and you knew your target's mail or IP address…"

"I see…Then you could set the send timer ahead of time, thus enabling you to have the desired signal arrive at the same time you shoot them in the game," Kikuoka replied, folding his bony fingers and resting his chin on top. "Let's assume that hurdle has been cleared. But you can't send some kind of fatal cursed bullet, only an ordinary stimulation signal within the bounds of the device."

"Meaning a sensation powerful enough to stop the heart… or a flavor, scent…sight, sound…Let's think about the senses in order. First is touch—the sense of the skin."

I traced my left palm with my index finger. I recalled the shock I felt earlier, when I found out the chocolate cake was actually ice cream.

"What if you sent a full-body chill, as cold as it can go? Like jumping into a giant ice bath. Could that cause the heart to stop?"

"Hmm…I thought that jumping into freezing water and causing the heart to stop was because the temperature difference makes all the veins contract, placing extra strain on the heart… right?"

"Okay, then that means this idea is out. The brain registering virtual cold wouldn't have an effect on the capillaries in your limbs, after all…"

"Then how about this?" Kikuoka asked, rubbing his hands together. He almost seemed to be gleeful. "You've got tiny insects…not beetles, more of the wormy kind, like caterpillars and millipedes. Someone creates the sensation of being packed into a hole squirming with these things. With visual, to boot. Brr, just imagining it is giving me goose bumps."

"…"

Against my will, I imagined the sensation.

Walking across a textured terrain, when suddenly the ground beneath my feet disappears, and I fall into a deep hole. Countless long, thin creatures squirm and wriggle, crawling against my skin and into the openings of my sleeves and collars…

"Yeah…that's pretty gross," I said, rubbing my arms, "but that's the kind of prank that happened during the Imagenerator virus. People got giant caterpillars and jellyfish dumped on their heads. But nobody's heart stopped…I think. Besides, when you're in a VRMMO, your subconscious is prepared for sudden events. Depending on your location, you can get surprised by a boss at any time. You can't play the game if your heart stops because of that stuff."

"That's a good point," Kikuoka said, shoulders drooping. He picked up his cup and swirled it.

"Next would be taste and smell. Let's say that your mouth was suddenly full of a terrible stench…like the taste of kiviak. Anyone who suffers that is going to try to vomit it out. Perhaps that gag reflex will affect their physical body…"

"Wouldn't that mean they died suffocating on vomit, rather than from cardiac arrest? And what's kiviak?"

I immediately regretted asking when I saw the sparkle in his eye. He loved talking about tasteless subjects. I suspected this was why he didn't have a girlfriend, despite his prestigious position.

"Oh, you've never heard of kiviak? It's an Inuit food. In early summer they catch these little birds called auks and stuff them inside of a hollowed-out seal. They leave the seal in a freezing location for several months. Eventually the seal's fat seeps into the auks and helps them ripen—well, rot. Once it's good and ready, they take the birds out and eat their innards, which have melted into a chocolaty substance. Apparently it's even smellier than the infamous surströmming, but once you get used to the taste, it's addictive..."

Thump! Our eyes were drawn to the side, where the two madams were on their feet, rushing away with their hands over their mouths. I sighed and interrupted Kikuoka.

"I'll be sure to try it the next time I'm in Greenland. Oh, and I don't need an explanation of what that sur-something is."

"Oh. Are you sure?"

"Don't look so disappointed. And I don't think even the smelliest food is going to cause someone's heart to stop. Let's go to the next sense: sight."

I took a hearty whiff of the coffee's fragrance to cleanse Kikuoka's tale of stench before continuing.

"Same as with the insect idea, I think stopping the heart with a meaningful image won't cut it, no matter how frightening or cruel the imagery is. Maybe if you dredged up some terrible trauma of the target's past, but I don't see how they could figure out what that would be."

"Hmm. You said 'meaningful.'"

"Yes. I remember reading about some incident that happened long before I was born, where a bunch of kids who were watching a cartoon on TV all passed out at the same time around the nation."

"Oh, that. I was in kindergarten at the time, so I saw it all happen," he said, thinking back fondly. "It was a scene where they alternated flashing blue and red lights, and it caused seizures."

"That's probably what I'm thinking of. You send a similar video with all kinds of extreme, exploding lights. Most people will shut their eyes on instinct, but you can't do that if the imagery is being pumped straight into the brain. Maybe that could cause some kind of shock to the system."

"Yes, you've got a point." Kikuoka nodded, then shook his head. "But that very problem was raised during the development of the AmuSphere. In the end, as a safety measure, they limited the output of the device. The AmuSphere can't generate visual output over a certain amplitude."

"All right, pal."

I glared directly at Kikuoka, my suspicion leveled up to a pure 100 percent.

"Are you really telling me you didn't already go over all of these possibilities before this? Why would you come to little old me after all the elite big shots in the Ministry of Internal Affairs put their heads together? What the hell is going on here?"

"No, no, it's not like that at all. Your ideas are very stimulating; they'll be a huge help to the process. Besides, I enjoy these conversations."

"Well, I don't. As for hearing, I'm guessing they have hardcoded limits on that, too. So that ends our talk. In conclusion: causing a player's heart to stop through in-game means is impossible. Death Gun's shooting and the two heart attacks are a simple coincidence. Now I'm leaving. Thanks for the food."

I had a feeling that allowing this conversation to continue would only lead to bad things, so I made to stand up and leave. But as I suspected, Kikuoka panicked and stopped me.

"Whoa, whoa, wait! I'm getting to the important part. You can order another slice of cake, just hang on for another minute."

"..."

"Anyway, I'm relieved that you arrived at that conclusion. I agree with you. Their deaths are not related to the in-game shooting. So here's my request..."

I knew I shouldn't have come, I told myself, waiting for what came next.

"Can you log in to *Gun Gale Online* and make contact with this Death Gun fellow?"

He grinned, as innocently and benignly as possible. I gave him my very coldest tone of voice in response.

"'Make contact'? Let's be honest, Mr. Kikuoka. You want me to go and get shot by this Death Gun."

"Ha-ha-ha, well, when you put it that way..."

"No! What if something happens to me? Why don't *you* get shot? See how you like having your heart stopped."

I tried to stand up again, but his arm shot out and caught my sleeve.

"Didn't we just come to the logical conclusion that it was impossible for that to happen? Besides, it seems that this Death Gun has an extremely rigid process in choosing his targets."

"...Process?" I asked, sitting down.

"Yes. Death Gun's two targets in the game, Zexceed and Usujio Tarako, were both well-known for their skills. In other words, I don't think he'll shoot you unless you're one of the best. I could spend years and never get to that point. But the man that even Akihiko Kayaba admitted was the best..."

"I can't do it, either! *GGO* isn't that easy of a game. There are tons of pros playing it."

"And what do you mean by that? You mentioned pros earlier, too."

I knew that I was falling right into his trap, but I explained anyway.

"It means exactly what it sounds like: people who earn a living playing the game. Of all the VRMMOs out there, *Gun Gale Online* is the only one with a game coin conversion system."

"...Oh?"

Even elite agent Kikuoka was not up on the full breadth of gaming lingo, and I could tell his confusion was not feigned this time.

"Basically, it's set up so that the cash you earn within the game can be withdrawn as actual money. It's an electronic currency, not actual yen, but it might as well be, since you can use it to buy anything you want already."

"But...how do they function as a business? I mean, I assume they're turning a profit on the game."

"Of course. Not all the players are actually earning money. It's like slots or horse racing. The monthly fee to play is three thousand yen, which is very high for a VRMMO. And the amount that an average player earns is maybe 10 percent of that...just a few hundred yen. But there's a high similarity to gambling in the game's system—every once in a while, someone gets a rare drop that's worth a ton of money. They sell that in the auction house and convert the earnings to electronic money—it can fetch them tens, even hundreds of thousands of yen. Anyone who hears that thinks...*Hey, that could be me.* There's even a giant casino inside the game."

"Ahh, I see..."

"The pros in *GGO* are the ones who earn a constant amount every month. The best players earn around two to three hundred thousand a month, which isn't that much in real-life terms... but it's enough for a frugal living. Basically, they're earning a kind of salary from the membership fees of the majority of the player base. That's what I meant when I said that the best in *GGO* get more hate and jealousy than in other games. They're like government employees scarfing down expensive cakes on the taxpayers' dime."

"Heh, you do have a way with words, Kirito. But that's what I like about you."

I ignored him and tried to steer the conversation to a conclusion.

"For that reason, high-level players in *GGO* put way more time and enthusiasm into the game than those in other MMOs. If I waltz in there without any knowledge of the game, I'm not going to get anywhere. Besides, as the name says, it's a gun-based game...and I'm not good at shooting systems. You'll need to find someone else."

"Hang on, hang on! I don't have any other options. In all honesty, you're the only VRMMO player I can actually contact in real life. Plus…if it's too difficult for you to take on the pros, why don't you turn it into a job as well?"

"…Huh?"

"I can pay you a stipend for research assistance. Let's say…the same amount one of those *GGO* pros makes in a month. This much."

He held up three fingers. I felt a lurch in my gut. That was enough to put together a new machine with a twenty-four-core CPU and have change to spare. But it also raised more questions.

"Something's not right, Mr. Kikuoka. Why are you so fixated on this case? First of all, I'm positive that this is just one of those weird occult stories that takes on a life of its own. Two people suffered heart failure and stopped showing up in-game, so the rest of the community made up a legend to explain it," I said flatly.

Kikuoka straightened his glasses with slender fingers, hiding his expression from me. He was clearly considering how much of the truth to reveal, and how much to keep hidden. A shrewd man, exactly as I thought.

"As a matter of fact, the bosses *are* worried about it." The bureaucrat was back to his usual smile. "The real-world influences of full-dive technology are under more scrutiny from a variety of fields than anything else. The social and cultural impact is undeniable, but the biological impact is hotly debated as well. They want to know how the human condition is changed by the virtual world. If it's determined that there is proper danger, it's possible that a move to regulate will be in the works again. As a matter of fact, there was almost proposed legislation on the matter right after the *SAO* Incident. But I, and the rest of the Virtual Division, feel that it would be wrong to hold back the tide now—for the sake of your generation, the ones enjoying these VRMMOs. I want to find the truth behind this odd series of events before it gets used for political purposes by those who want to crack down on the technology. If it turns out to be total nonsense, that's the best outcome. I want to be sure of that. What do you think?"

"Given your understanding of young people playing VR games, I'll choose to interpret your position as being altruistic. But if you're really that worried about it, why not go through the actual companies involved? Consulting their logs should tell you who shot Zexceed and Tarako. Even if the registration data within the game is nonsense, you could get an IP address and contact the provider to learn the real name and address."

"I've got a long reach, but not long enough to cross the Pacific." Kikuoka's bitter expression didn't look feigned this time.

"The developer of *Gun Gale Online* is a company called Zaskar...Actually, I don't even know if they're a proper company, but at any rate, the servers are based in America. They've got excellent customer support in-game, but their actual office location, phone number, and e-mail address are all private. I swear, ever since The Seed was unveiled, these VR worlds pop up like bamboo shoots."

"...Oh, really."

I looked disappointed, but kept my cards close to my chest—only Agil and I knew the origin of the VRMMO development suite known as The Seed. As far as the rest of the world knew, the replica of Aincrad that appeared in the new *ALfheim Online* was simply left behind on the old *SAO* server that the late RCT Progress inherited.

"So basically, if we want to get down to the truth of the matter, we've got to make direct contact in-game. Of course, we'll take every precaution we can in the name of safety. You'll dive from a room we've prepared for you, with a full-time monitor that will automatically disconnect the AmuSphere if its output does anything funny. I'm not asking you to get shot; I just want you to react based on what you see and how you feel. So...are you in?"

I realized that the noose was completely around my neck. There was no getting out of this one.

Regretting my decision to come, I also couldn't deny that my interest was getting piqued. The power to affect the real world from the virtual world…If such a thing existed, could that be the beginning of the world-changing power that Akihiko Kayaba sought? Was the incident that began on a cold winter day three years ago still ongoing…?

If that was the case, maybe I did have a responsibility to see this unfold.

I shut my eyes, let out a deep breath, and said, "All right. I don't like being railroaded into this, but I'll do it. But I can't make any guarantees I'll be able to find this Death Gun guy. We don't even know if he's real."

"Ah, yes…about that." Kikuoka smiled, all innocence. "Didn't I tell you? One of the players present at the first shooting got an audio log of the room. He brought a compressed version of it to us. It's Death Gun's voice. Have a listen."

He extended a wireless earbud to me. *I hope your heart stops next*, I thought as I eyed him suspiciously.

"…How considerate of you—thanks," I said instead.

I stuck the bud in my ear and watched Kikuoka tap at the screen. A low buzz of excitement sounded in my ears. Suddenly, the murmuring stopped. A piercing statement cut through the tense silence.

"This is the true power, the true strength! Carve this name and the terror it commands into your hearts, you fools! My name, and the name of my weapon, is…*Death Gun!!*"

The voice was strangely metallic and inhuman. And yet I vividly felt the flesh-and-blood human presence beyond that shout. It was the voice of someone not role-playing, but channeling a true impulse to slaughter.

2

Get off at Exit C-10 of the Chiyoda Line, in Otemachi Station. Glance at watch, on left hand.

Five minutes left until three in the afternoon. Asuna Yuuki was about to lower her hand when she caught the date in the little windows in the watch face.

Sunday, December 7, 2025.

It was not a special date or anniversary. But something meaningful and emotional filled Asuna's chest. She raised her head and began walking down Eitai Street in the direction of the Imperial Palace and thought to herself:

Very soon, it'll be a year...

She didn't bother to include the other part of that sentence: *...since I came back to this world.*

Asuna had gone from the iron fortress of *SAO* to the birdcage of *ALO* before she was finally freed into reality in the middle of January. What happened to her in the virtual world was slowly shifting from recent experience to more distant memory, but there were moments like this when she was filled with wonder that she was actually in the real world.

The orderly placement of paving stones in the wide street. The rustling of the trees as the chill wind brushed them. The passing crowds, faces tucked into coat lapels or scarves. And Asuna herself, as she passed through this flow.

These were not 3D objects modeled with digital code, but real minerals, plants, animals.

But what did *real* mean, anyway? If it meant "clusters of atoms and molecules," then they were no different from those virtual polygons. The polygons were real, they just existed in the memory banks of a server somewhere. The only difference was the type of particles they were.

Was it just a matter of reversibility? Everything in the real world, organic or not, could not be restored to its previous state if destroyed. But objects in the virtual world could be replicated from the same information down to the very last byte.

...No.

That was not necessarily the case. In Aincrad, there had been loss, unrecoverable and permanent. The things that Asuna had touched, felt, gained, and lost in those two years in the virtual castle were undoubtedly real.

But if that was the case...

"...What is the difference between the real world...and the virtual world...?" she mumbled to herself.

"Only the amount of information," came the answer from right next to her. She jumped up with a start.

"Wh-wha?!"

She turned to see a boy, blinking in surprise.

Longish bangs in front. Slender, fine features with just a hint of sharpness. A plain black shirt with a black leather jacket and faded black jeans.

It was so close to the look of his old avatar that it seemed strange not to see sword pommels over his shoulders. Asuna took a deep breath to sooth the sweet, lonely pain in her breast, and beamed.

"...Oh, you startled me. You came out of nowhere! Did you use a teleport crystal or something?"

Kazuto Kirigaya smiled wryly.

"I didn't come out of nowhere. I made it to the meeting place just in the nick of time."

"Huh...?"

She looked around and realized he was right.

The gentle afternoon sun warmed the street and glittered off the surface of the moat. The bridge just ahead led to a heavily guarded gate. They were just before the gate to the Imperial Palace, as Kazuto had suggested. She'd been lost in thought as she walked, and came upon their meeting place without even realizing it.

Asuna's grin turned shy and she shrugged.

"Ha-ha, I guess I was on autopilot. So, um...hello, Kirito."

"Better watch out, there's no nav function in real life. Hey, Asuna."

Their greetings exchanged, Kazuto suddenly narrowed his eyes and stared at her.

"Wh-what's up?" she asked, arms crossed in front of her.

Kazuto hastily shook his head and mumbled, "Er, um... well...just thinking, that outfit looks good on you. Makes me remember..."

"Huh...?"

She looked down at her clothes, and in two seconds, Asuna understood what he meant.

She was wearing a coat for the first time this winter: white tweed, with an ivory white knit sweater and a red skirt that sported an argyle pattern.

In other words, she had dressed herself in the colors of the old Knights of the Blood guild. It occurred to her that she'd probably worn that white-and-red knight's uniform nearly every day in Aincrad. No doubt Kazuto was reminded of those times by her outfit today.

She ran her left hand up and down her waist and grinned again.

"...You're right. I don't have the rapier, though. And I can't help but notice you've chosen black for yourself, Kirito."

He smiled bashfully. "I don't have the dual blades, though.

I usually do a better job of avoiding an all-black outfit, but Sugu washed all of my clothes this morning, so this was all I had to wear."

"That's what happens when you let your laundry pile up," she noted, jabbing him disapprovingly on the shoulder, then slipping her hand around his arm.

"So it just so happens that we're both in our old colors today. What are the odds?" she asked, looking up just slightly so she could see into his eyes. He coughed gently and answered without much emotion.

"Well, if we keep meeting up regularly for a year, such things will happen eventually."

"Oh, come on! You're supposed to say, 'I know, right?' not get all logical on me!" She pursed her lips and tugged on his jacket sleeve. "C'mon, let's not just stand around here all day. It's going to get dark soon."

"Um, yeah."

She sidled up next to him and started crossing the bridge over the waterway.

The imperial gate, white and traditional, was lit by the already reddish western sun, throwing black shadows over the bridge. Though it was a Sunday, the cold weather kept the tourist crowds away.

They passed a police officer in a heavy coat and went through the gate to a little checkpoint, where they took plastic entrance tickets. After the silver fence they were in the midst of a tiny woods so peaceful, it was hard to believe they were smack in the center of Tokyo.

It was Asuna's idea to go somewhere on Sunday, but it was Kazuto's suggestion that they meet outside the Imperial Palace gate.

The palace itself was off-limits, of course, but the northeast section of the East Garden, which was within the moat's ring, was actually open to the public on Sundays—a fact that Asuna didn't know until today. Naturally, it was her first time visiting.

As they made their way along the wide path, she was struck by a sudden curiosity, and turned to the boy at her right.

"Why did you choose the palace as our date spot, anyway? Are you actually a history buff?"

"Um, not really. The main reason was...well, because I was just busy with an errand nearby before this..."

He snorted briefly, remembering something, then returned to his ordinary gentle smile.

"I'll tell you more about that later, but for now, don't you think the Imperial Palace is kind of a fascinating place?"

"...Fascinating? How so?" she wondered. He reached out with his right hand and pointed at the thick trees surrounding them.

"It's about one and a quarter miles north to south, and just under a mile east to west. If you add in Kitanomaru Park and the outer gardens, the total area is about 1.3 square miles, which is twenty percent of Chiyoda Ward all on its own. It's way larger than the Vatican or Buckingham Palace, though not as big as Versailles. It's not just the size, though—there are no subways or tunnels underneath it, and a no-fly zone over it. Basically, this is like one giant vertical area of no-entry smack in the middle of Tokyo."

A map of Tokyo materialized in Asuna's mind. She spun her finger around in the air absently as she thought, then nodded in understanding.

"Now that I think about it, the major highways around the center of the city are either circular routes or radial routes stretching outward. I guess this must be the center around which they all stretch..."

"Exactly. Tokyo isn't a grid pattern like Kyoto, it's a city built in concentric circles. And the very center of it is completely shut off from the rest, not just physically, but also insofar as information. In a way, it's like the World Tree in the old *ALO*...oops. Didn't mean to drudge up bad memories."

"It's okay, I'm fine."

Asuna had been trapped for many months atop the giant tree at the center of that world. She shook her head to show that it was all right and asked, "I understand that it's physically off-limits…but what do you mean, informationally?"

"Oh, well…"

Kazuto looked around the woods, and briefly pointed out a few spots.

"See the security cameras there, there, and over there? That's a completely stand-alone security system. There's a closed network here with zero connections to the outside."

"Ohh…And they're rather strangely shaped cameras, too, aren't they?"

Kazuto's finger was pointing to a pole, atop which sat a black sphere. If he hadn't pointed it out, she would have assumed it was just a light pole.

"I've heard they're testing out next-gen security tech here…At any rate, it's smack in the middle of Tokyo, but it's also its own little isolated world. That's a fancy way of putting it, though."

"Ha-ha, just a bit."

As they talked, the path wound around an enormous stone wall and rose up a sudden hill. They walked in silence for a few moments and the view opened up before them. Over the wall was an enormous grassy field so large it was hazy. The grass was dried and dead in the midwinter cold, and the trees around it had lost all of their leaves, but it was sure to be a splendid sight in the spring.

"This is where the old Edo Castle used to be. The great hall that you see in all those historical dramas was apparently on the northern end of that grass field."

"Let's go see!"

Asuna squeezed Kazuto's hand and picked up her pace. There were still very few other visitors, and nearly all of them were foreign tourists. On the way, they were stopped by a couple with two adorable blonde daughters, asking for a picture to be taken, so Kazuto politely obliged. The wife offered to take a picture of them in exchange, so they bashfully lined up for a photo of their own.

Once the photo file was sent to their phones, they waved good-bye to the little girls. As the family walked away into the orange setting sun, Asuna heaved a heavy sigh.

"...You tired?" Kazuto asked. She shot him a dirty look.

"Ab-so-lute-ly not! I was just thinking about us being like that in the fut...erm...Oh, forget it!"

Her cheeks burned when she realized what she was about to say, and raced ahead.

"H-hey, wait up!"

She and Kazuto raced a short distance until they reached the little path that split the field into north and south. They found a bench near a fork in the path, and plopped down.

She still had her head turned away from him in a huff. Eventually, he found something to say.

"Well, um...I'm sure Yui would be happy to have a little sister."

Despite the fresh rush of blood to her face at such a direct acknowledgment, Asuna couldn't help but chuckle.

"Y-yeah, right."

"What? Why would you laugh? That's mean..."

"Ha-ha, sorry, sorry. It's really a shame that we can't live with Yui over here, too..."

Yui was the name of a girl they'd met on the old *SAO* server. In reality, she was just a mental health counseling program—an AI—but she accepted Asuna as her mother and Kazuto as her father. As Aincrad was collapsing around them, Kazuto managed to sneak her core program out in his NerveGear so that she didn't get deleted with everything else. Now she "lived" in a desktop PC Kazuto had prepared just for her in his room.

But the only way they could interact with her directly was within a full dive—in other words, within *ALO*. They could contact her in the real world using their cell phones, but that was limited by battery power, and wasn't the same as being "with" her.

No matter how much Asuna loved Yui as a daughter, and no

matter how much Yui loved Asuna as a mother, there was always a wall between them—the wall that separated the real world and the virtual world.

Kazuto suddenly squeezed her hand.

"It's all right. We'll be able to live with her someday, once full-dive tech evolves more, and augmented reality functions are commonplace."

"Yeah...I'm...I'm sure you're right."

"As time goes on, the distinction between reality and the virtual world will get even more blurry. The only major wall between us right now is the amount of information..."

She savored Kazuto's words and squeezed his hand firmly, then looked up.

"You mentioned that earlier, Kirito. Something about the difference between the real world and virtual world being the amount of information. What does that mean?"

"Well..."

His eyes wandered for a moment, then glanced down at their hands, intertwined atop the bench.

"There's still a difference between holding our hands like this in reality, and doing the exact same thing in *ALO*, you know?"

Asuna concentrated on the sensation of her left hand.

The pressure of the palm pressing against hers. The warmth that kept away the winter chill. Those sensations still existed between the fairy avatars of *ALfheim Online*. But even the most advanced full-dive technology couldn't replicate the adhesion that seemed to suck the skin together, the friction of the fingerprints, and the faint pulse of blood flowing through the veins.

"Yeah, you're right...You still feel more with your real hands. So that's what you mean by 'the amount of information'?"

"Yes. But as the AmuSphere evolves and becomes able to emulate skin sensations and pulsing, what then? Will you be able to tell the difference between a real hand and an avatar's hand just by touch?"

"I will," Asuna said instantly. Kazuto blinked in surprise. She stared directly at him as she added, "I'll be able to recognize your hand, at least. Probably not other people's."

In that moment, the temperature of Kazuto's hand rose slightly, and its pulse quickened. She grinned in satisfaction.

"There's still more information you get in reality from all the senses, not just touch: sights, sounds, flavors, and smells. So... even if the current AmuSphere gets AR functionality..."

"I know. The instant you see or touch something, you'll know if it's real or not."

AR, or augmented reality, was a feature that would use the AmuSphere to combine digital information with the user's real vision and hearing. If that became possible, there would be no need for desktop PCs or cell phones anymore. You could display a virtual desktop in front of your eyes, browse the web and send e-mail, even navigate roads and attach info tags to people or objects. The possibilities were endless.

For the moment, RCT and the other major IT manufacturers were hard at work, but there were still major barriers to usability—the electron pulses went out of focus with the movement of the body, extra batteries were required, and so on.

"Sadly, there are people who think constant AR will never be applicable with the current headgear model. But I'm sure that if there's a breakthrough on the technical end, and we can get massive sensory data here in the real world...we might be able to experience an instant full dive without lying in bed while plugged into a wall."

Asuna nodded and continued where he left off.

"Then we can cross the wall between worlds and be with Yui all the time. I'm sure that day will come."

"Yeah, it will."

Oddly enough, the words they exchanged were nearly the same as what they said after leaving Yui behind on the twenty-second floor of Aincrad. When Asuna realized this, something warm flooded into her heart, and she rested her head on Kazuto's shoulder.

The promise of that reunion was fulfilled just months later.

So what they said just now was sure to come true as well.

As close as they were to the winter solstice, the sun plummeted behind the trees to the west as if it had been dropped. Birds flocked against the brilliant red sky as they returned to their nests.

Centuries ago, the people living in the castle here atop this vast grassy field must have looked up at the same sunset. Centuries later, freed from the flow of time, would someone look upon the same red sky...?

"Ahhh..."

Asuna murmured, feeling a nostalgic, melancholic urge escaping her breast. Kazuto looked over at her. Their eyes met, and she smiled.

"I think I understand why you brought me here."

"Uh...y-you do?"

"Yes. If the world is built from the axis of time and the plane of space, then the center of Tokyo, the real world where we live now, is this place right here. And the central axis of the virtual world, which is even now expanding thanks to The Seed, was that old castle. That's why the color of this sunset feels so nostalgic..."

Kazuto blinked a few times, then beamed widely.

"I see...Yeah, good point. Actually, I hadn't thought about it that hard. But...what you just said did help me realize one thing."

"What's that?"

"The shape of Aincrad. Maybe that spherical cone shape was meant to be a symbol of the axis of time and plane of space."

Asuna thought it over and eventually agreed.

"Yes...maybe you're right. But if that's the case, the world that our guild leader sought to create eventually tapers down to a point and disappears. At least, until a certain someone blew the entire thing up."

"G-geez, I'm sorry...Vice Commander."

They shared a silent chuckle. A few seconds later, Kazuto sucked in a deep breath and stood up from the bench, still holding her hand.

"Well, time to get going. This place closes at five."

"Okay. We should bring Liz and Leafa next time. I bet it would be fun to have a picnic on the grass."

"Yeah. Maybe in the spring."

Using his grip to get to her feet, Asuna took one last look at the sunset in all directions.

She wanted to go home. Not to the Yuuki household, in the Miyasaka neighborhood of Setagaya Ward. To their little forest cottage that had temporarily existed on the twenty-second floor of the old Aincrad.

The little log cabin was obliterated in the destruction of the floating castle, but Asuna had a secret plan percolating in her heart. Until that plan came to fruition, the room they rented in Yggdrasil City atop the World Tree in *Alfheim* was home to her, Kirito, and Yui.

As they walked toward Hirakawa Gate on the north end, Asuna turned to Kazuto and asked, "Can you log in tonight? I want to tell Yui about what we just talked about."

"Yeah, sure. Is ten o'clock okay?" he answered with a smile. It was soon wiped away.

"What's wrong? Do you have something else to do?"

"No, it's not that. I'm pretty sure I can do it tonight, but... actually, Asuna..."

It was rare for him to be at a loss for words like that. He mumbled for a few seconds, but what he said next froze Asuna's heart with fear.

"...Pretty soon, I might be converting my *ALO* Kirito to a different game..."

"...Wh-what?!" she screamed. Startled, a few birds took off from a nearby branch.

3

Dusk.

The low-hanging clouds were painted yellow by the tilt of the setting sun.

The shadows of the ruined high-rise buildings, remnants of the former age, steadily grew across the wasteland of rock and sand. If she was going to be on standby for another hour, she'd have to think about switching to her nighttime loadout.

Sinon didn't like fighting with night-vision goggles, because it diminished the tension of that kill-or-be-killed mentality. She sighed atop the shadowed concrete, wishing the party that was her target would show up before the sunlight disappeared. The other five people in the depressing ambush with Sinon had to be thinking the same thing.

As if to give voice to the entire party, an attacker, with his small-caliber submachine gun at his waist, grumbled, "Damn, how long are we gonna be waiting here...? Hey, Dyne, you sure they're coming? The lead wasn't a bust, was it?"

Dyne, the craggy, burly leader of the squadron, shook his head. The large assault rifle hanging from his shoulder clattered.

"They've been hunting the same route, same time, nearly every day for three weeks. I've confirmed it all myself. They're a little late on the return today, but it's probably just because the mob spawn rate's a little higher than usual, and they're cleaning up more of 'em. We'll get better rewards for it, so don't complain."

"Yeah, but," the man in front pouted, "today's target is the same group we attacked last week, right? Won't be they be on guard and change their route…?"

"It's been six days since our last ambush. And they've been visiting the exact same hunting ground every time. Their squadron's built for mob hunting…"

Dyne's lips curled into a mocking smile.

"No matter how many times they get attacked and lose their earnings, they'll just keep trying to make it up by hunting more. The perfect prey for a manhunting squadron like us. We can pull this off another two or three times; you'll see."

"I dunno if I can believe that. Anyone's going to put together a plan after they get attacked the first time."

"Maybe they'd be on the lookout the day after, but they'll forget soon enough. Field mob algorithms are the same every day. After a while, they get to be just as robotic and automatic as the monsters they kill. Weak losers—no pride at all."

Sinon buried her face deeper into her muffler, disgusted by the conversation. The presence of emotions only dulled one's trigger finger, yet she couldn't prevent her irritation at Dyne's boastful gloating.

Apparently Dyne felt that parties who hunted mobs on a routine were lower than him, a PvPer, yet lying in wait to ambush the same party over and over had no effect whatsoever on his pride. If they were going to spend hours in wait here on neutral ground, they could have earned a lot more fighting another high-level squadron in the underground ruins.

Naturally, that increased the chance that they'd die and respawn in town without their equipment. But that was battle. Only trial by fire truly disciplined the soul.

She'd been working with Dyne's squadron for the last two weeks. She regretted the decision to join almost immediately. Despite their proud claims of fighting only other players, they were a safety-first party, only setting their sights on inferior opponents and disengaging at the very first sign of danger.

But Sinon raised no complaints about the focus of the squadron. She followed Dyne's orders and pulled the trigger when she was supposed to. She wasn't trying to make a name for herself through loyalty. She wanted to be sure that when she faced off against Dyne as an enemy, she had as much data and knowledge as possible to land the perfect head shot.

While she had nothing good to say about his personality, Dyne's eighteenth-place finish in the last Bullet of Bullets and the rare SIG SG 550 assault rifle that sprayed 5.56 mm rounds were the real deal. So she shut her mouth, kept her eyes bright, and absorbed all of the information he carelessly dispersed.

Dyne blathered on.

"...The thing is, they've all got optical guns for hunting mobs, so they can't arrange for live-ammo guns for the entire group on a whim. At best, they might have one for covering fire, but no more. And Sinon's got her sniper rifle to help take out whoever uses that one. There's absolutely no flaw in our plan. Right, Sinon?"

Sinon barely nodded with her face still stuffed in the muffler, suddenly the unwanted focus of the conversation. She did not speak up, hoping that would indicate she didn't want any part of it.

Dyne snorted in annoyance, while the attacker grinned at her and said, "Yeah, that makes sense. With Sinon's long-distance fire, we've still got the advantage. By the way, Sinocchi..."

He crawled over toward her, never leaving the shade of their cover, the lazy smile still plastered on his face.

"You got any time later? I was hoping to raise my Sniping skill and I could use a few pointers. Feel like getting a cup of tea?"

Sinon glanced quickly at the weapon on his waist. His main weapon was an H&K UMP, a live-ammo submachine gun. He played an Agility-first build, so his evasion in a head-on battle was notable, but level-wise and equipment-wise, he was not worth remembering. She wracked her brains to recall his name and dipped her head.

"I'm sorry, Ginrou. I've got something to do IRL later..."

Her voice was high-pitched, clear and adorable, not at all like her real voice. Sinon felt sick to her stomach; this was why she hated talking. Despite the fact that she'd just turned him down, Ginrou's leering smile did not vanish from his lips. A subsection of the male players in the game seemed to feel some kind of pleasure from hearing her voice. The skin of her back crawled at the thought.

The first time she dove into the VRMMORPG *Gun Gale Online*, she chose a bland, crude male body for her avatar. When the game made it immediately known that switching genders from player to character was not allowed, she wanted to pick as tall, muscular, and soldierlike a body as possible.

Instead, the randomly generated body was that of a petite, fragile, doll-like little girl. When she made to delete her account and build a new character, the friend who had invited her to try the game said it would be "such a waste" to get rid of it right away, and eventually she leveled the character up to the point that it really *would* have been a waste to start over.

Because of that, she had to deal with the occasional unwanted offer like this. Sinon played to fight, not to deal with this nonsense.

"Oh, right, you're a student in real life, aren't you, Sinocchi? College? Got a report to write?"

"...Yeah, sure..."

It felt like after she'd accidentally admitted something about school when logging off one day, the come-ons had gotten much more insistent. She could never admit that she was actually in high school.

The other two front-line players, who had been fiddling with their menus through all of this, finally approached to keep Ginrou away. One of them, a man with green bangs that hung over his smoke-styled goggles, said, "Ginrou, can't you see you're bothering her? Don't bring up RL."

"Yeah. Just because you've been playing solo here and in real life for years doesn't mean you have to bug her," said the other man, who had a camouflage helmet tilted at a rakish angle. Ginrou knuckled both of their heads.

"Like either of you have had a girlfriend in years!"

The three of them cackled and Sinon scrunched up even smaller in disbelief.

If you played *GGO* to battle against other players, there were much better ways to spend your downtime—maintaining focus, checking equipment, and the like. If you were trying to earn enough in-game money to cash out, you were better off in a mob-hunting squadron. And if you wanted to meet people, even among the gender-fixed games, there were much more fantastical worlds with a better gender ratio than this miserable, blasted ruin of a landscape. What did these people think they were doing here?

She buried her face back in the muffler and traced her fingers along the massive rifle barrel, propped up on its bipod.

Someday, I will destroy your avatars with this gun. Will you still be laughing and bothering me then?

Her foul mood was absorbed by the chill of the barrel, and slowly subsided.

"Here they come."

The last member of the party, spying with binoculars through a hole in the collapsed concrete wall, announced the presence of their target a full twenty minutes later.

The three attackers and Dyne stopped chatting at once, and the mood in the air turned serious.

Sinon glanced up at the sky. The yellow clouds were taking on a tiny bit of red, but there was plenty of light left.

"Finally decided to show up," Dyne growled softly. He leaned forward and took the binoculars from the scout at the wall. He peered through the same hole, checking the status of the enemy for himself.

"...Yep, that's them. Seven...that's one more than last week. Four in front with optical blasters. One with a large-bore laser rifle. Plus...ooh, one with a Minimi. That one had an optic last week, so they must've switched over to live ammo in response. If you're gonna snipe anyone, that's the one. Last one's...wearing a cloak, so I can't see a weapon..."

Sinon lay flat and pressed her face to her rifle's high-power scope. Their group of six was lying in wait in a ruined building from the old civilization; the building sat on a hill with some vantage over the surrounding terrain. The ragged concrete walls and steel rebar skeletons made for good cover, and the view made it perfect for surveying the wasteland ahead.

She looked up to the sky again to ensure that the virtual sun would not reflect in her lens, then flipped up the scope covers, front and rear.

With her right eye pressed to the lens and the scope set to the lowest magnification, she could see small dots moving across the landscape. She tweaked the magnification dial with her fingertips. With each click of the dial, the little black sesame-seed dots grew until she saw seven players.

As Dyne said, four of them had optical assault guns, two of which were constantly checking their surroundings with binoculars of their own. But unless the group had nearly mastered the Search skill, they would not find Sinon's squadron lying in wait.

In the middle of the pack were two players with large guns on their shoulders. One had a semiautomatic optical laser rifle, while the other had a live-ammo light machine gun, the FN Minimi. In real life, that was an excellent squad infantry support weapon—even the Japanese Self-Defense Force used it. Indeed, because over half the power of the optical gun attacks would be neutralized by their defensive field, it was the Minimi that posed the most threat by far.

There were two main types of weapons in *Gun Gale Online*: live-ammo guns and optical guns. Live ammo delivered plenty of damage per round and could penetrate defensive fields. But they also required the user to lug around heavy ammo clips, and bullet trajectories were susceptible to the effects of wind and humidity.

Meanwhile, optical guns were much lighter to carry, and featured longer range and higher precision. The energy packs that served as clips were much more compact as well, but the strength of the guns was diminished by the defensive fields that players wore as armor.

Therefore, it was common wisdom that optical guns were better against monsters, while live-ammo guns were better suited for human players. But there was another feature that distinguished the two categories.

All the optical guns were designed from scratch with fictional names, but the live-ammo guns were based directly on actual, existing firearms. Therefore all the gun fanatics—such as Dyne and Ginrou—who made up a significant portion of the *GGO* player base happily preferred to carry around live-ammunition guns, only switching to optics when hunting monsters.

The rifle Sinon had her cheek pressed against was also a live-ammo gun. But before she'd come to this game, Sinon couldn't have told you a single gun manufacturer. She learned their names as items within the game, but she had not developed even the slightest bit of interest in learning more about their real-life counterparts. To her, the unlimited number of guns in the world of *GGO* were nothing more than 3D-modeled objects, and she didn't even like the thought of seeing a real gun in the regular world.

All she did was destroy her virtual enemies with virtual bullets in this land of slaughter—until her heart turned hard as stone, and her blood cold as ice.

Sinon would pull the trigger again today to keep that process in motion.

She swept aside any unnecessary thoughts and budged the rifle slightly. At the back of the enemy formation was a player wearing enormous face-covering goggles and a large camouflage cloak. As Dyne had said, the player's equipment was hidden.

He was extremely large. There must have been a hefty backpack slung over his shoulders, because the cloak bulged alarmingly over his back. The hands peeking out of his sleeves were empty. Whatever weapon hung from his waist, it couldn't be any larger than a submachine gun.

"Can't see his face because of the cloak?" Ginrou's voice floated up from behind. He spoke in a joking tone, but there was no hiding the note of tension. "Think it's him? You know...Death Gun."

"Hah! Like he exists," Dyne snorted. "Besides, didn't they say that guy was short, and wearing a ghillie suit? This one's huge. Six feet at a minimum. I'm thinking he must be a Strength-build hauler. He's carrying their loot haul, ammo, and energy packs in that bag. Probably doesn't have anything decent to shoot with. Ignore him in combat."

Sinon watched the man through her scope.

The heavy goggles hid his expression. Only his mouth was exposed. The lips were tightly shut and absolutely still. The other members, though on guard, seemed to be chatting—she caught the occasional flash of white teeth—but the large man in the back was completely silent. There was no wavering in his silent march.

Half a year of experience in *GGO* taught Sinon's instincts that this man was the true threat, much more than the one with the Minimi. But aside from the backpack, there were no other obvious bulges in his cloak. Perhaps he was hiding a small but high-powered elite weapon. But anything that good and that small would have to be an optical gun, and not powerful enough to make the difference in PvP. Perhaps the pressure she felt emanating from him was her imagination...

After some hesitation, Sinon spoke up in a soft voice.

"I get a bad feeling from him. I want to snipe the guy in the cloak first."

Dyne pulled the binoculars away and looked at her, eyebrow cocked.

"Why? He's barely got any gear on."

"...I have no proof. I just don't like him being such an uncertain variable."

"If that's the case, shouldn't the Minimi be the obvious variable to worry about? If the blasters sneak up on us while you're still getting rid of that one, we'll have trouble on our hands."

While protection fields were effective against optical guns, their benefit lessened as the distance between gun and target shrank. At very close range, it was quite possible for a laser blaster with its much larger magazine to overpower the alternative. Sinon had no leg to stand on, so she withdrew her opinion.

"...All right. First target is the Minimi. If possible, I'll take the cloak with my next shot."

The problem was that when it came to sniping, the only truly effective shot came before the target knew it was under attack. Once the enemy knew where she was firing from, evasion was as simple as staying out of her line of fire.

"Hey, no more time to talk. Distance of 2,500," said the recon man, who had taken the binoculars back from Dyne. The leader nodded and turned to the three attackers behind him.

"All right. We're going to follow the plan, move up to the shadow of the building ahead, and wait for them. Sinon, once we're on the move, we won't be able to see them, so you need to alert us if anything changes. I'll give you the signal to snipe."

"Roger."

Sinon put her eye back to the rifle scope. Nothing had changed in the party. They still marched across the wasteland, their pace slow and easy.

As the scout had said, two and a half kilometers separated Sinon's squadron from the enemy. Just slightly closer than halfway in between, an even larger ruined building loomed over the landscape. Dyne and the rest were going to use that as cover and ambush their prey as they approached.

"All right, move out," Dyne commanded. Aside from Sinon, the others muttered quick acknowledgments. Their boots scraped on the gravelly sand as they slid down the backside of the sloping hill. Sinon waited for the whistling evening wind to drown out their footsteps, then pulled out a small headset from below her muffler and affixed it to her left ear.

For the next few minutes, Sinon would be fighting the sniper's lonely battle against pressure. The next bullet she fired would have an enormous influence on the fight that ensued. The only things she could rely on were her trigger finger and the silent gun. She rubbed the massive barrel with her left hand. The black metal answered her with chilly silence.

More than anything else, it was this gun that had cemented Sinon's infamy in this world as a very rare type of sniper. It was called a PGM Ultima Ratio Hecate II. At four and a half feet long and just over thirty pounds, it fired enormous .50-caliber (12.7 mm) rounds.

In the real world, from what she'd heard, it was categorized as an antimateriel sniper rifle, meant for piercing military vehicles or structures. It was so powerful that some fancy-named treaty prohibited it from being used against human targets. There was no such law here.

She'd earned it three months ago, around the time she was experienced enough to be considered a veteran of *GGO*. On a whim, she'd been playing solo in a massive ruined dungeon beneath the capital city SBC Glocken when she fell into a chute trap.

Gun Gale Online took place after a massive war in the distant past caused civilization to collapse, and the players were the descendants of space colonies who had returned to Earth. Glocken itself was the giant ship they'd used to reach the planet, and beneath the ship was the ruin of one of the giant cities that had been wiped out in the war. The city's ruins were crawling with automatic fighter drones and genetically modified creatures that greeted the adventurers, who dreamed of unearthing ancient treasures. Sinon fell right into the bottom level of that dungeon, its most deadly region.

It was not the kind of place a solo player should be able to handle. Soon she had resigned herself to dying in the very first encounter and spawning back at the save point in town. Eventually, she ended up in a huge, stadiumlike round space, which featured an extremely grotesque creature.

Based on the size and name, it appeared to be a boss monster, but she had never seen it on any of the news sites or wikis. Upon this realization, what little of a gamer's soul Sinon had was stimulated into action. If she was going to die, she'd die fighting this thing. She hid in the exhaust vents over the stadium and trained her rifle on the beast.

The battle did not turn out as she expected. The boss had a number of attack styles—heat ray, claws, poisonous gas—but the range of all these attacks was just short enough to miss her position. Meanwhile, Sinon's rifle did paltry amounts of damage to a target that was barely within its effective range. Based on the stock of ammo she was carrying, it would be impossible for her to beat the creature unless she hit its weak forehead with essentially every bullet she had remaining.

With ice-cold calculation and concentration, Sinon pulled it off. The boss collapsed and exploded into vanishing shards three hours after the battle began.

What it dropped was an enormous rifle she'd never seen before. By design, both NPC and player craftsmen could not forge powerful live-ammo guns, and the only ones for sale in town were low power models. If you wanted anything midlevel or higher, the only option was excavating them from ruins. The Ultima Ratio Hecate II that Sinon found was in the very rarest tier of excavated weapons.

It was said that there were only ten antimaterial rifles on the server, including Sinon's Hecate II. They commanded an extraordinary price on the market, of course—the last one to be auctioned off went for twenty mega-credits, or twenty million credits. The exchange rate of credits to yen was a hundred to one, meaning the player had earned about 200,000 yen for the sale.

Sinon was a high school student living alone and stretching her monthly budget as far as it could humanly go, so she was sorely tempted by that number. Recently she'd been earning enough to pay 1,500 yen, half the cost of her monthly subscription, but that was still half of her allowance. And if she dove any more often than she already did, she couldn't maintain her grades. But 200,000 yen was enough to cover all the money she'd sunk into the game with a majority to spare.

Yet Sinon did not sell the gun. Making money wasn't the reason she played *GGO*; it was to defeat her enemies—every player stronger than her—so she could conquer her own weakness. And on top of that, for the first time ever, she felt a *soul* within that simple item.

Because of the Hecate II's massive bulk, it required a considerable amount of strength to carry. Fortunately for Sinon, she'd spent more of her stat points on Strength than Agility, and she just barely met the required value. The first time she brought it into battle and caught an enemy in its scope, she felt strength and will within the heavy, cold pile of metal. It was a cruel soul that desired slaughter and demanded death. It was every bit the unflinching, unyielding, unsentimental being that Sinon wished herself to be.

Much later, she learned that the name Hecate came from the Greek goddess of the underworld. That was the moment she decided this gun would be her first, and last, partner.

The party continued to move through her scope finder.

Sinon lifted her head and looked down on the wasteland directly to see that Dyne's group of five was approaching the large building that separated her and the target. The distance between the two was already down to 700 meters—under half a mile. She put her eye back to the scope and waited for Dyne's order.

Less than a minute later, a crackling voice came through the earpiece.

"We're in position."

"Roger that. Target hasn't changed course or speed. Distance to you, 400. Distance to me, 1,500."

"They're still a ways off. Are you ready?" he asked.

She gave him a bland affirmative.

"...Okay. Begin sniping."

"Roger."

Their conversation over, Sinon held her mouth shut and placed her right index finger against the trigger guard.

Through the scope, she saw her first target, the man with the Minimi on his shoulder, saying something as he walked. In last week's battle, Sinon had not been on sniping duty, but had charged into battle with an assault rifle. She surely would have seen him at such a close range, but she didn't remember his face. Based on his support weapon, however, he must have been at a considerable level.

She moved the reticle delicately, trying to stifle the increased pulse of her heart. Correcting for distance, wind direction, and the target's movement speed, she placed her aim over a yard in the air to the upper left of the man. Her finger traced the trigger.

In that instant, a translucent, light green sphere appeared in her field of vision.

The sphere, shifting and wavering periodically, covered from the center of the man's chest to around his knees. It was called a "bullet circle," an offensive assistance system that only Sinon could see. When the bullet left the gun, it would land at a random point within the circle. At its current size, the amount of the circle occupied by the man's body was about a third, meaning she had a 30 percent chance of hitting the target. On top of that, even with the power of the Hecate II, it was impossible to get an instant kill by hitting the limbs alone, which dropped her chances of a one-hit kill even lower.

The size of the bullet circle was affected by distance, the gun's stats, the weather, the amount of light, and the player's skill and stat values, but the most important parameter of all of them was the shooter's pulse.

The AmuSphere monitored her real-life heart rate as she lay on the bed, sending that information to the game engine. The instant her heart thumped, the circle expanded to its maximum size. Then it would shrink and shrink until the next heartbeat pushed it out again. If a sniper wanted to raise her accuracy, she had to pull the trigger in the space between heartbeats.

The problem was that a relaxed, resting heart rate might be sixty BPM, one per second, but under the stress of sniping, that could rise to twice the speed, causing the circle to expand and contract wildly. Under those circumstances, it was impossible to time the shot between pulses.

This was the main reason there were so few snipers in *GGO*.

You couldn't land a hit. There was no way to eliminate tension when sniping. The heart rate had an effect in close combat as well, of course, but at that distance even an affected shot could land at times—especially with fully automatic SMGs and assault rifles. But when sniping a target over half a mile away, the bullet circle expanded to several times the size of a person. The fact that Sinon had gotten this one to a 30 percent accuracy size was nothing short of a miracle.

But, Sinon thought to herself, *how bad is that pressure, that anxiety, that fear, when you really get down to it? Fifteen hundred meters? That's like making a basket with a wadded-up piece of paper. It's not that bad—*

Not compared to what happened back then.

Her head went ice-cold. Her heart was as still as if it never beat.

Ice. I am a machine of coldest ice.

The pitch of the bullet circle's shifting dropped precipitously. Her sense of time slowed until she could easily, clearly, identify the moment the circle was at its smallest size.

One…two…three times the circle shrank, and when it covered only the heart of the man lugging the Minimi on his shoulder, Sinon pulled the trigger.

The world shook with a blast like thunder.

A gout of fire erupted from the muzzle brake on the end of the

Hecate II's barrel, and the projectile burst forward faster than the sound of the blast. The recoil pushed the rifle and Sinon herself backward, but she held firm with both feet.

Beneath her reticle, the man looked up, perhaps noticing the muzzle flash in the distance. His gaze met hers through the scope.

And in that very instant, the man's chest, shoulder and head exploded into tiny shards and disappeared. Just a moment later, the rest of his body crumbled into nothing, like a broken glass statue. Unfortunately for him, the extremely expensive-looking Minimi on his shoulder was selected as a random drop and fell into the sand. When he rematerialized back in town, he'd be hit by the double shock of a one-hit fatality and the loss of his gear.

Sinon observed all of the above without emotion. Her right hand moved automatically, pulling the Hecate II's bolt handle. It spit out an impressively sized cartridge, which hit a nearby rock with a heavy clang and vanished.

Even as she loaded the next round, Sinon adjusted the rifle to the right, catching her secondary target, the large cloaked man, in the sight. His goggled face was pointed straight at her. She placed the sight just above his body and brushed the trigger. The green projection circle appeared again and instantly shrank to a point.

Three seconds had passed since the first bullet left the gun. A semiautomatic rifle could continue firing, but the bolt-action Hecate II was not that convenient. However, your average player, upon the shock and momentary petrification of seeing his partner's body exploding, needed at least five seconds to mentally recover, identify the firing direction, and begin taking evasive maneuvers. She figured that with the ensuing chaos, she'd have time to succeed at a second shot.

But the cloaked man showed not a single sign of panic. He stared straight at Sinon through his large goggles. He had to be a serious veteran, probably a player whose name others would recognize. She pulled the trigger.

At this point, the man would be seeing a pale, translucent red "bullet line" that indicated the arc of incoming enemy fire. This defensive aid was implemented to increase the fun of the gunfights, augmenting the guessing game of when and where an attack would come from. Bold players with excellent reflexes and high Agility could evade more than half the bullets from an automatic assault rifle at a distance of fifty yards.

The greatest benefit to playing the sniper class was that the very first shot did not cause the bullet line to appear to the target. Since Sinon had already taken her first shot and revealed her location, that advantage was now lost.

There was another roar. The Hecate II's bullet, a missile of pure death launched by her unfeeling finger, ripped through the pale yellow atmosphere.

As Sinon feared, the man calmly took one wide step to the right. The next instant, the 12.7 mm round tore through the space several feet away. A large circular mass disappeared from a concrete wall jutting up out of the wasteland far behind him.

Sinon's hand moved automatically to the bolt to load the next bullet, but she did not return her finger to the trigger.

Any further sniping would be pointless. If she wanted to hit her target, she needed to move locations, hide from his line of sight, and wait out the sixty seconds for the recognition system to reset and allow her that first sneak attack again. But by then, the battle would essentially be decided. She whispered into the com next to her mouth, eye still pressed to the scope.

"First target clear. Second target failed."

Dyne's response was immediate.

"Roger that. Begin attack…Go, go, go!!"

Sinon heard the faint scrape of boots hitting ground through the com. She hissed the breath she'd been holding in.

Her duty was over. The Hecate II was an extremely valuable gun, so charging into close battle with it could be disastrous if she died and it was dropped for the enemy to claim. Dyne told her that she could wait on standby after her job was done. She wasn't happy that her second shot missed, but all she could do now was pray that the bad feeling she had was an illusion.

Despite knowing her role was done, Sinon moved the rifle again and bumped down the magnification on the scope to get a view of the entire enemy squadron. The four lead gunners were scrambling toward rocks and concrete walls for cover, while in the back, the man with the large laser and the cloaked—

"Ah!"

She gasped. The large man had just thrown his arms up and ripped away the camouflage cloak. There were no weapons in his hands. Or at his waist.

The bulky object on his back, which she'd taken to be a backpack for hauling items, was exposed at last.

A metal rail curved from shoulder to broad shoulder. Hanging from it was a delicately framed metallic object.

It was a spherical machine cradled in a Y-shaped frame. At the top was a thick carrying handle, and below that, a bundle of six gun barrels. It was easily over three feet long. There was a belt feeder affixed to the machine, which was connected to a high-capacity ammo belt that also hung from the frame.

This dreadful thing, too enormous and menacing to be called a "gun," itched at Sinon's memory. She had seen this weapon once in an index on a *GGO* fansite.

It was called a GE M134 minigun, and belonged to the Heavy Machine Gun category—the largest type of weapons found in *Gun Gale Online*. Those six barrels rotated at high speed, loading, firing, and expelling cartridges nearly instantly. It could fire a hundred 7.62 mm bullets in a *single second*, making it more than worthy of its demonic reputation. This was not just a gun—it was a war machine.

Naturally, such a thing was tremendously heavy. From what she recalled, the body alone weighed forty pounds, and with that much ammo, the whole thing had to be pushing ninety. Even the most extreme STR-heavy build couldn't fit all of that under the personal weight limit. He had to be suffering a movement penalty for overencumbrance.

The squadron wasn't moving slowly because their hunt went long. They were going at the maximum speed that man could move.

Stunned, Sinon watched through the scope as the large man reached around his back to grab the handle of the minigun. The massive machine slid smoothly across the rail and rotated ninety degrees to point forward when it reached his right side. He planted his legs wide, pointed the six-barreled gun forward, and for the first time, the mouth below his goggles curved into a triumphant smile.

She hurriedly spun the scope's dial to the minimum magnification. In the bottom left of her view, Ginrou and the two other attackers were charging in with submachine guns. The enemy party's front-line shooters were firing back with laser blasters, but the pale blue lasers all fizzled out and vanished into a rippling waterlike surface about three feet in front of her teammates. The anti-optical defense fields were doing their job.

Their live-ammo SMGs spit return fire, and one of the targets, caught a little too far out from his rock cover, flailed with a few red hit blips and collapsed. Ginrou's group charged farther, up to the closest concrete wall between them and their targets.

The large man squatted. His minigun spun into life, spraying a brilliant curtain of bullets for just a third of a second.

That was all it took to obliterate both the concrete cover and Ginrou's avatar. He was as helpless as a sand sculpture hit by a tidal wave.

"…"

Sinon bit her lip and stood up. She lifted the Hecate II off the ground, folded its bipod, and wrapped the ammo belt around her body.

At four and a half feet, the gun was nearly as long as Sinon was tall, since she was at just over five feet herself. It bit hard into her shoulder, but was still within her carrying capacity. The only reasons she could manage to keep the tiny H&K MP7 as a sidearm without going over the limit were her considerable Strength stat and the fact that the only Hecate ammo she had were the seven bullets in the magazine.

Even by the naked eye, she could see the muzzle flashes of the gunfight happening nearly a mile away. Sinon silently sprinted as fast as she could go.

At present, Dyne's team was at a severe disadvantage. Against just the one man with the minigun, they could win by maintaining medium distance and keeping light on their feet. But with the others and their laser blasters at close enough proximity to negate their protective fields, they had no choice but to tackle the nearer enemy.

Though she was part of the squadron, they would not complain if Sinon simply retreated to safety. She had a duty in their mission, and she did her part.

And yet she ran straight for the battle. Not because she wanted to save her companions—it was that confident grin on the minigunner's face that drove her forward.

He had the strength and ability to laugh on the battlefield. He'd played long enough to earn himself a minigun, which was at least as rare as the Hecate, if not moreso. He had the patience to build up the frightful amount of strength necessary to wield it. And he had the willpower to react to Sinon's sniping calmly and precisely.

Only by fighting and killing such a foe could Sinon eliminate the other, weaker her—the young Shino Asada, who was always crying in a heap inside her mind.

That was the only reason she continued to challenge this world of madness. If she ran away for safety now, she would be ruining everything she'd built so far.

Sinon raced on through the dusty air, her feet carrying her as quickly across the dried earth as her stats allowed.

She avoided the rocks and ruined walls that stuck out of the gravelly sand here and there, launching herself over obstacles if necessary, and in barely a minute, she was within proximity of the battle.

It was a mad, direct dash, using every ounce of her Agility. She didn't spare a single thought to hiding herself. The enemy probably knew she was approaching already.

The area of trading fire had moved quite a bit since the battle began. Naturally, it was Dyne's group that was being pushed. With the minigun's commanding fire pinning the group, the enemy's front troopers were able to close the distance. In order to stay out of the effective range of their lasers, Dyne and the others had to keep darting from cover to cover.

She was close enough now that her direct sprint would no longer work. If she traveled in the open, the minigun would pulverize her with a hail of bullets. Worse, there were almost no more of the concrete walls the team had been using as cover in the direction they were fleeing. The only thing left was the half-collapsed building they'd used to approach as they staged the ambush. Once they ran in there, they'd be trapped like rats.

Noticing all of these details at once, Sinon leaped straight for the shadow of the wall behind which Dyne and the others were hiding. As soon as she got closer, three pale, translucent red lines popped into being right in front of her.

"Ugh!"

She gritted her teeth and entered an evasive maneuver. Those were the bullet lines that showed the trajectories of the enemy attackers' laser blasters.

First she crouched as low as she could go to duck the first of the bullet lines. The next instant, a pale blue laser burned the air over her head. The second line was just before her eyes. She immediately launched off her right foot as hard as she could, floating through the air. The laser passed just below her stomach, leaving her vision pure white for an instant.

The third bullet line intersected her airborne trajectory at a slightly higher point. She shrunk her head down as much as she could and avoided the hit, but the beam caught her light blue hair right at the tip, sending little sparking bits of light flying.

Having successfully dodged all three laser blasts, Sinon landed back on the ground to see—

—a terrifyingly thick red line the color of blood and over a foot across. It had to be the bullet line of the minigun. That deluge of bullets would be upon her in less than a second.

Lashing her terrified body into action, she tensed the foot that just hit the ground and launched herself airborne again. Twisting in midair, she tilted herself backward like a high-jumper.

The next moment, she felt a ferocious flow of energy storm just past the skin of her back. The white, gleaming swarm of bullets passed through her field of vision and tore huge chunks out of the already pockmarked ruined building behind them.

Just before she could land flat on her back onto the sand, Sinon flipped over and stopped herself with hands and feet. At the same time, she tossed her body forward. After a few somersaults, she reached the shadow of the wall where Dyne and the others hid.

The squadron leader stared at the sudden appearance of Sinon with open shock. No matter how charitably she interpreted the look, it was clearly not the shine of appreciation for unexpected reinforcement, but disbelief that anyone would rush to their death like this.

Dyne quickly broke his gaze and looked down at the assault rifle in his hands. When he spoke, his voice was ragged and quiet.

"...They hired a bodyguard."

"Bodyguard?"

"Don't you know him? That muscle-bound freak with the minigun is Behemoth. He makes his base on the north continent. Works as a so-called bodyguard for squadrons with more money than balls."

That's a much more respectable play style than what you do, Sinon thought, but she didn't share that opinion with him. She glanced over at the three other attackers, who were occasionally popping their heads out from cover and mounting weak attempts at counterfire, and spoke just loud enough for all of them to hear.

"If we stay hidden here, we'll be wiped out in no time. The minigun should be running out of ammo soon, and if we all attack at once, he might rethink that strafing fire. That's the only chance we'll have to get rid of him. You two with the SMGs from the left, Dyne and me from the right, and the M4 back here to cover us..."

Dyne interrupted her hoarsely.

"It won't work. They've still got three blasters left. If we charge in, our fields won't last..."

"Automatic blaster fire isn't as fast as live rounds. We can dodge half of them."

"We can't!" he repeated, shaking his head. "The minigun will just tear us to shreds. I hate to say it, but we should give up. Better to log out now and give them the satisfaction of victory than suffer the consequences..."

In a neutral zone, logging out didn't happen immediately. The soulless avatar would sit in place for several minutes, open to any kind of attack. There was even the low possibility that weapons or armor would drop randomly once the avatar was dead.

She'd always thought that Dyne's orders to pull back came too soon, but she never expected this kind of cowardly capitulation. He was like a sulking child throwing a tantrum. Sinon stared straight at his face, the picture of a hardened soldier. He gritted his teeth and wailed.

"What? Don't get all serious about a stupid game! It's the same thing, we're either going to die here or die charging them..."

"Then die!" she spit back at him. "Show me you at least have the guts to look down the barrel of a gun and die, even if it's 'just a stupid game'!"

What was she doing yelling at this man who was nothing more than a mark, a future target to be eliminated? Her time with this squadron was obviously at its end.

But despite all of that, she grabbed the lapel of Dyne's camo jacket and yanked him up. At the same time, she hissed orders at the three wide-eyed members beside them.

"Just distract the minigun for three seconds and I'll pick him off with the Hecate."

"...Y-you got it," stammered the attacker with the goggles and green hair. The other two nodded after his lead.

"Good. We'll split in two and charge from both directions at the same time."

Sinon shoved the sulking Dyne's waist over to the far edge of their cover. She drew her MP7 sidearm and held out her fingers to count down.

Three, two, one.

"Go!!"

They leaped as one into the sandy battlefield, where death waited a second away with automatic fire.

Multiple bullet lines immediately crossed her path. She doubled over and slid to avoid them, looking up to catch sight of the enemy squadron.

About sixty feet ahead and to the right, two laser blasters waited on the other side of a wall. Farther to the left was another. Behemoth, the minigunner, was in the middle and another ten yards behind, trying to get a bead on the two allies who'd darted left.

Sinon ran to her right, pointing the MP7 at the blasters. A bullet circle appeared when she squeezed the trigger, but her heart rate was too high to control, and it pulsed and bounced over the attackers' bodies.

She fired anyway. The recoil on the SMG was almost nothing compared to the Hecate II. In no time at all, the twenty-round magazine of 4.6 mm bullets was empty.

The two men with blasters panicked despite her wild firing and ducked back behind the wall. A few of the bullets hit them, not enough to take their HP down, but enough to buy her a few seconds of time.

"Cover me, Dyne!" she shouted, crumpling to the ground and pulling the Hecate II off her back and into her arms. There was no time to set up the bipod. She had to balance its tremendous weight as she found the scope.

The magnification was still set low, but Behemoth's upper half filled the viewfinder. He was looking straight at her. Sinon didn't have time to wait for the trajectory circle to shrink—she pulled the trigger.

With a blast, her desperate shot ripped through the air right next to Behemoth's head. He stumbled with the shock of its passing, the goggles flying off his face and crumbling into nothing.

Missed!

She bit her lip and tried to stand, but her gaze caught Behemoth's through the scope. His face exposed, Behemoth's gray eyes flashed threateningly. His lips still had that confident grin.

An enormous red light swallowed Sinon's entire body.

Instantly she knew there was no way to avoid it. There was no time to stand out of her firing crouch and leap to either side.

But she could at least face the gun head-on.

Sinon got up and stared straight at Behemoth, intending to honor her challenge. Abruptly, a few lights sparkled on his giant frame.

It was Dyne. He had his assault rifle in firing position with one knee on the ground, carefully taking his shot. Getting *anything* to hit him at this range and in this situation was an admirable display of skill, even if she didn't think much of his personality. Sinon jumped hard to her right. Several dozen bullets passed through the space where her body had just been.

"Dyne! Move to the ri—"

Before she could finish that sentence, the two behind the wall opened fire on Dyne as he got back to his feet.

They were too close. The beams burned through his protective field and then his body.

He looked at Sinon for an instant, then turned to face forward.

"Raaah!!"

And charged straight ahead.

A storm of lasers fired back at him. He dodged, weaved, and tore onward. But he couldn't evade all of them.

With his last few seconds, Dyne pulled a plasma grenade that hung from his belt like a good-luck charm and heaved it over the wall. With his HP down to zero, the avatar exploded into virtual shards, his back to Sinon.

The next moment, a flash turned the entire world white.

There was a tremendous shock, like some Norse god's hammer striking the earth. Pale energy coursed through the ground, throwing up waves of sand. One of the attackers flew into the air, disintegrating before he even hit the ground.

Nice one!

With a silent cheer for the departed Dyne, Sinon squinted her eyes against the wave of sand and scanned the scene.

One of the two allies who'd charged the minigunner on the left was already gone, but so was the other enemy blaster on that side. On the right flank, Dyne had engaged in a virtual suicide attack, taking one of the two enemies down with him and leaving the other stunned for a time.

And there, hazy through the thick clouds of airborne dust, was a large silhouette making its way straight for her.

At this point, it was essentially a one-on-one fight between Behemoth and Sinon. But a heavy machine gun vs. sniper rifle fight at this distance was completely one-sided.

She had to find cover to protect herself from the minigun while she prepared to fire. But with a simple head-to-head situation, there was no way to hide or take it by surprise…

No, wait.

She held her breath. While the sand still hung heavy in the air from Dyne's grenade, Behemoth wouldn't be able to pinpoint her exact location. She couldn't snipe him, either, of course, but she might able to move to the one spot in this area where his gun's hail of fire couldn't reach her.

As soon as the idea occurred to her, she was off and running.

The tattered remains of the large building loomed just behind the area where they were fighting.

Once Sinon was through the entrance, the yellow sky could be seen clearly through the collapsed rear half of the building. She found what she wanted on the right-hand wall—stairs upward. She moved as quickly as she could without kicking over any of the detritus littering the ground and making noise.

The metal staircase was missing the occasional step, but it wasn't enough to stop her quick ascent. She practically kicked the wall of the landing to shift directions and continue upward.

In less than twenty seconds she had reached the fifth floor, where the stairs stopped. There was a large window to her left.

Here she could buy the few seconds necessary to take sniping position without drawing Behemoth's attention. She pressed the stock of the Hecate against her shoulder and looked out the window.

Immediately, her vision went red.

On the ground over a dozen yards below, Behemoth already had the minigun pointed up as far as it could go, trained perfectly on Sinon. He read her like a book—her plan, her execution, everything.

She didn't have time to retreat or hide.

He was too good. A real *GGO* player—a soldier.

But that was the exact kind of opponent Sinon wanted. She would kill him. She had to.

There was no hesitation. She put her right foot on the windowsill, not bothering to take firing position, and launched herself upward.

A burning, brilliant stream of energy tore upward from the ground. A tremendous shock smashed through Sinon's left knee. Her leg tore away, taking a massive chunk of her HP bar with it.

But she was still alive. Sinon floated through the air over the minigun's trajectory of fire. Straight over the head of Behemoth.

He tilted backward, trying to catch up to the angle of her flight before his clip ran out. But he couldn't get to her. The minigun was connected to the frame on his back and couldn't point directly upward.

As her body began to descend, Sinon pressed the Hecate's stock to her shoulder and looked through the scope. All she saw was Behemoth's burly features. At last, the smile was gone from his lips. His teeth were bared, and his eyes burned on the fuel of shock and anger.

Sinon was barely conscious of the movement of her own mouth.

As if taking over from him, she smiled. A fierce, cruel, cold smile.

Falling a great height was hardly the ideal position for steady sniping, but she was too close to miss. When the tip of the barrel was just three feet from his head, the green bullet circle shrank into place in the center of his face.

"The End," she muttered, and pulled the trigger.

A spear of light shot out of the fingertip of the goddess of the underworld, bearing the maximum amount of energy of any bullet in this world.

It ripped a hole from his face through his trunk and buried itself deep in the gravelly earth.

The next instant, an explosive shock wave erupted outward, and Behemoth's body blew apart from the inside.

4

The moment she left the school gate, a cold, dry wind buffeted her cheeks.

Shino Asada stopped still and adjusted her sand-yellow muffler.

With over half of her face covered by the cloth and the other half by her plastic-rimmed glasses, Shino was ready to continue walking. Her heart itched steadily as she strode quickly down the leaf-strewn path.

...Out of the 680 days of her high school education, 156 were finished.

She was a quarter of the way done. In that sense, the length of her torture was astounding. But if she included middle school in the total, nearly 60 percent of the trial was in the past. *It'll end someday...It will end someday.* She repeated it like a magic spell.

Of course, even when she reached her high school graduation, she had no goals to achieve or career to seek. She just wanted to be free of the "high school" affiliation that she was largely forced to accept.

Every day she visited that prison, listened to lifeless lectures from her teachers, and participated in gym and other activities with students who hadn't evolved a bit since they were toddlers. Shino wondered what the point of all of it was. On very rare occasions, there was a teacher with a worthwhile lesson, or a fellow student with admirable qualities, but their existences were hardly necessary to Shino.

Once, Shino told her grandparents—who were her legal guardians—that rather than go to high school, she would prefer to start working immediately, or go to an occupational school to prepare for a career. Her old-fashioned grandfather went red with rage, and her grandmother wept, saying that she needed to go to a good school and marry into a good family, or else they would be doing her father a disservice. Left without a choice, Shino studied hard and got into a fairly good municipal school in Tokyo. Upon starting there, she was surprised to find no real difference from the public middle school back home.

So, as she did each day of middle school, every afternoon after she left the school gates, Shino performed her ritual of counting down the days.

Shino's solitary apartment was about halfway between the JR train station and school. It was a cramped place, the main room less than a hundred square feet with a small kitchen, but it was adjacent to a shopping arcade, which was convenient.

At three thirty in the afternoon, the arcade street was relatively uncrowded.

Shino stopped first at the display table of the bookstore and noticed a new book from one of her favorite authors, but it was in hardcover, so she decided to hold off. If she put in a reservation online, she'd be able to rent it from the local library in a month or so.

Next she bought an eraser and a graph-paper notebook at a stationery store, checked her remaining cash, and made her way to the supermarket at the center of the shopping district. Shino's dinners were always extremely simple, so as long as her meal balanced nutrition, calories, and price, she didn't care what it looked or tasted like.

She was passing by the video arcade next to the market, planning on a carrot and celery soup with tofu cubes, when someone called her name.

"Asada!"

It came from the narrow alleyway between the two buildings. She automatically tensed and slowly rotated ninety degrees to her right.

In the alley were three girls wearing the same school uniform as Shino, but with considerable differences in the length of their skirts. One was squatting down and fiddling with her phone, while the other two leaned against the wall of the supermarket and leered at Shino.

She stood there without responding until one of the two leaners arrogantly beckoned her over with a wave of her head.

"Come here."

Shino didn't move.

"...What do you want?"

The other one quickly strode over and grabbed Shino by the wrist.

"Just get over here."

She had no choice but to be pulled along. They shoved her back down to the far end of the alley, well out of sight from the main walkway, where the squatting student looked up at her. She was Endou, the leader of the trio. With her black eyeliner, slanted eyes, and pointy chin, she looked like some kind of predatory insect.

Endou's glitter-sparkling lips twisted menacingly. "Hey, Asada. We were just doing a ton of karaoke, and now we can't afford the train fare home. We'll pay you back tomorrow if you lend us this much."

She held up a finger. She didn't want 100 yen, or 1,000. That meant 10,000.

Shino silently thought of a number of logical rebuttals to this demand—how could they have sung a "ton" of karaoke in the twenty minutes since school let out? Why did they need train fare when all three of them had passes? Why did they need 10,000 yen just to ride the train? But none of these questions would change her fate.

It was the second time this trio had demanded money from her. The last time, she claimed she didn't have that much. Shino figured that excuse wouldn't fly a second time, but she tried anyway.

"Of course I don't have that much."

For an instant, Endou's smile disappeared, then returned.

"Then go withdraw some cash."

"…"

Shino tried to walk back out to the street without responding. They weren't going to follow her to a bank where people would be watching, and nobody was stupid enough to wander back into trouble once they were in the clear. But Endou wasn't done.

"Leave your bag. And your wallet. All you'll need is your card, right?"

Shino stopped and turned back. Endou was still smiling, but her narrowed eyes glinted like a cat toying with its prey.

At one point, she'd actually thought these three were her friends. Shino cursed her own stupidity.

Shino was fresh to Tokyo from the country when school started, so she didn't know anyone and had nothing in common to discuss with anyone. It was Endou's group who reached out to her first.

They invited her to eat lunch, and eventually the four of them would stop to get fast food after school. Shino mostly listened, and occasionally found herself irritated by the topics, but she still appreciated the gesture. At last, she had friends that didn't know about *what happened*. At least she could be a normal student here.

It wasn't until much, much later that she realized they'd singled her out because they checked her address in the class registry and figured out she lived alone.

When they asked if they could come visit, Shino gladly accepted. The girls praised her apartment, raved jealously about it, and they sat chatting and snacking until it got dark.

The girls came to Shino's apartment the next day as well. And the day after that.

Soon the three of them came to her place to change outfits and then take the train for a night on the town. They would leave their belongings in the apartment, and soon the closet was stuffed with the girls' clothes.

Shoes. Bags. Cosmetics. Endou's and her friends' items grew and grew. By May, the three were often stumbling back drunk and sleeping in the one-room apartment with her.

One day, near her breaking point, Shino timidly pointed out that with the way they visited every day, she had no time or ability to study.

Endou's only answer was, "Aren't we friends?" The next day, she demanded a spare key.

Then, on the last Saturday of May, Shino came back to her door from the library to hear raucous laughter coming from inside. It wasn't just Endou and the two others.

She held her breath and listened intently. The fact that she had to go to these lengths over the state of her own apartment filled her with misery.

There were clearly several men in her apartment.

Unfamiliar men in her home. Shino collapsed with fear. Then came rage. She understood the truth at last.

She walked down the stairs of the building and called the police. The officer who responded was quite confused by the testimony from both sides, but Shino stayed firm and said she didn't know any of them.

When the officer insisted that she report to the station with him, Endou glared at Shino in fury, said, "I see how it is," then gathered up her things and left.

Her vengeance came swift.

Endou exhibited a demonic ability for research that was unthinkable given her typical demeanor. She looked up the reason Shino was living alone—an incident that had occurred in a distant prefecture five years ago, the details of which could barely be found on the Net anymore—and revealed it to the entire school. None of the students talked to her anymore, and even the teachers avoided looking at her.

Everything went back to the way it was in middle school.

But Shino was fine with that.

It was her weakness, her desire for friends, that had clouded her judgment. She was the only one who could save herself. She had to get stronger on her own, heal the scars of the past on her own. She didn't need friends for that. Enemies were better. Enemies for her to fight. Everything around her was an enemy.

Shino held a deep breath and stared Endou in the eyes.

There was a dangerous glint in those narrowed slits. Endou's smile vanished for good.

She growled, "What? Get going."

"No."

"...Huh?"

"No. I'm not giving you money," Shino said, eyes locked.

Firm refusal would only bring more hostility and harassment. But Shino certainly wasn't going to give in to their demands, and she didn't want to pretend to go along with it and run off, either. She hated the idea of exposing her own weakness, not to Endou, but to herself. She'd lived the last five years wanting to be stronger. If she crumbled now, that effort would have gone to waste.

"What...? You think this is funny?"

Endou took a step forward, her right eyelid twitching. The other two quickly circled around Shino's back and leaned in close.

"I'm leaving now. Get out of the way," Shino said quietly. She knew that no matter how menacing an air they might affect, Endou's trio didn't have the guts to turn that into action. They were relatively good girls when they went back home. After the last incident that involved the police, they'd learned their lesson about that.

But.

Endou knew Shino's weakness—the sore point that would bleed if prodded.

Her brightly colored lips twisted into a mocking smile. Endou held up her fist and pointed it at the bridge of Shino's glasses. The index and middle fingers extended outward into the universal child's symbol of a gun, a harmless caricature.

But that gesture was all it took to cast a chill over Shino's entire body.

Her legs gradually lost strength. Her sense of balance abandoned her. The color drained from the alleyway. She couldn't take her eyes off the glittering fingernails trained directly on her face. As her heart rate rose, so did a high-pitched whine in her ears...

"*Bang!*" Endou shouted. A pitiful shriek squeaked out of Shino's throat. Her body trembled uncontrollably.

"Ka-hah...Listen, Asada"—Endou chuckled, fingers still held in position—"my big brother has a couple of model guns. Maybe I'll bring them to school sometime. You like pistols, don't you?"

"..."

Her tongue wouldn't move. It was shrunken and useless inside her desiccated mouth.

Shino shook her head, trembling. If she saw an actual model gun in class, she might pass out on the spot. Just imagining the picture made her stomach churn. She doubled over.

"Don't start puking, Asada!" said a pleased voice from behind her.

"That time you barfed and passed out in history class was a real headache to clean up."

"Then again, it's nothing you don't see around here with old drunk guys."

High-pitched giggling.

She wanted to get away. To run and never look back. But she couldn't do that. The two opposing voices in her head ranted on.

"Look, just give me what you have on you and I'll cut you some slack. You don't look too good, after all."

Endou reached out for the bag in Shino's hand, but she couldn't resist. The more she told herself not to think about it, not to remember, the more the black glimmer came back on the movie screen of her memory. The feeling of that heavy, slick metal. The pungent smell of gunpowder tickling her nose.

Somewhere behind them, a voice shouted.

"This way, Officer! Hurry!"

It belonged to a young man.

Endou's hand instantly left her bag. The three bullies burst off running toward the exit and melted into the crowd milling through the arcade.

Shino's strength truly left her now, and she fell to her knees. Her focus was fixed entirely on controlling her breathing and preventing the onset of a panic attack. Eventually the sounds of the bustling shoppers and the wafting smell of grilled chicken outside the supermarket returned to her senses. The nightmare flashback was fading.

She must have sat there for most of a minute. Eventually the voice returned, hesitant.

"Um…are you all right, Asada?"

Shino took one deep breath and put some strength into her wilted legs to stand. She turned and straightened her glasses to see a short, skinny boy.

He wore jeans and a nylon parka, with a dark green daypack on his shoulder. His rounded face had a black baseball cap on top. In his personal clothes, he simply looked like a middle schooler. Only the dark, sunken bags around his eyes belied his youthful appearance.

Shino knew this boy's name. He was the only person in this city she could trust, the only person who wasn't an enemy, and a good battle comrade in her other world.

Sensing that her palpitations were finally under control, Shino gave him a weak smile.

"…I'm all right. Thank you, Shinkawa. Where's the officer?"

She looked around him, but the dim alleyway was still empty, and it didn't seem like anyone was about to show up.

Kyouji Shinkawa scratched the back of his cap and grinned.

"That was a bluff. They do that all the time in TV shows and manga, right? I always wanted to try it—I'm glad it worked."

"…"

Shino shook her head in disbelief.

"…I can't believe you thought to pull off a stunt like that on the spot. Why are you here?"

"Oh, I was just over at the game arcade. I left out of the back entrance, and…"

He turned around and pointed. There was indeed a small gray door set in the middle of the stained concrete wall.

"I saw them surrounding you. Almost called the cops for real, but then I had that idea instead…"

"No, you did great. Thanks."

She smiled again, and for a moment Kyouji's face crumpled into a grin before returning to a worried expression.

"Um, does this…happen a lot? I mean, I know it's not technically my business…but maybe you should inform the school…"

"That's not going to be any help. Don't worry, if it actually escalates higher than it is now, I'll go straight to the police. Besides, don't fret about me…What about you?"

"Oh…I'm fine. I'm not going to see them anymore," the slender boy said, his smile tinged with self-deprecation.

Kyouji Shinkawa had been Shino's classmate until summer vacation. He hadn't been to school since the start of the semester.

From what the rumors said, Kyouji had undergone severe hazing at the hands of the upperclassmen in his soccer club. His small size and his wealthy family's clinic made him the perfect target. Though they hadn't been as carelessly blatant about it as Endou's group, they'd apparently sucked him dry of a

preposterous sum of money through meals and other entertainment. But Kyouji had never told her the truth directly.

They'd first met at the local library back in June.

Shino had been looking through a large comparison graph in a book titled *Firearms of the World*. At the time, she'd gotten to the point where looking at photos of guns didn't cause her to have panic attacks. But when she got to the page with The Gun on it, she could only look at it for ten seconds before slamming the book shut. At that exact moment, someone spoke up behind her back.

"Do you like guns?"

It was several moments before she realized he was a member of her class.

Shino was about to instantly and firmly declare that it wasn't true—in fact, it was just the opposite—but then he would wonder why she was looking through such a book, and she didn't think she could come up with a logical answer for that question. So, her response was ambiguous.

These days, Kyouji knew that Shino suffered from a terrible phobia of guns. But at the time, he misconstrued her answer and excitedly sat down next to her.

He pointed out the various guns on the graph and dropped pieces of knowledge on each of them. Shino let him speak, trying to hide her alarm, but eventually he reached the topic of another world he visited.

She knew that full-dive game machines had come to market a few years ago, and had even heard the term *VRMMO* before. But Shino had no familiarity with video games as a child, and assumed that the world of swords and sorcery were best left to fantasy novels.

But the virtual world that Kyouji described to her on their first meeting did not contain any swords or magic spells. It had guns.

This world's name was *Gun Gale Online*. It was a brutal wasteland in which players slaughtered one another with incredibly detailed models of actual guns.

Shino cut him off and asked in a quiet voice, "Does this game have a gun called…?"

The boy blinked in surprise, then nodded as if the answer should have been obvious.

She wondered to herself if she might be able to face The Gun again in the virtual world. Another chance to come across, fight against, and perhaps finally get past the black gun that had left deep, permanent scars on her heart five years ago, at the age of eleven…

Shino clenched hands cold with sweat and asked Kyouji another question, her throat ragged. How much did she need to play this game?

That was half a year ago.

The girl named Sinon who existed within Shino was now a ruthless sniper who terrorized the wastes of *GGO*. Sadly, she had not yet encountered a foe who wielded The Gun. And because of that, her question remained. Was she, Shino Asada—not Sinon—truly any stronger in the real world…?

The answer was still beyond her grasp.

"…You want to get something to drink? I'll buy," Kyouji asked.

Shino was pulled back to reality. She looked up to see that what little light made it into the narrow alley was starting to redden.

"…Really?" She smiled and Kyouji nodded happily.

"Tell me more about that huge fight you had. There's a quiet little café through the back street here."

A few minutes later, seated in the back of the café with a cup of fragrant milk tea in her hands, Shino finally felt relaxed. Endou's gang would be after her again soon, but she could worry about that when the time came.

"I heard about your big battle the other day. Seems you were quite the hero."

She looked up and saw the skinny boy poking at the scoop of vanilla ice cream in his iced coffee with a spoon and staring at her.

"…It's not true. The entire operation was a failure. We lost four out of our six squadron members. Given that we were the ones waiting in ambush, that's hardly what you'd call a victory."

Imagining a real gun while in reality was more than enough to trigger a panic attack for Shino, but thanks to the virtual rehabilitation program that was *GGO*, discussing the game in real life gave her enough stability to remain calm.

"Still, it was amazing. Apparently Behemoth has never died in a group battle like that before."

"Oh…I didn't realize he was so famous. I never saw his name in the Bullet of Bullets rankings."

"Of course not. Doesn't matter how powerful your minigun is if the weight of five hundred bullets puts you way over the limit and you can't run. The BoB's an every-man-for-himself fight, so once someone picks you off from a distance, that's it. But in a group battle with adequate backup, he's basically invincible. That gun's not fair, it really isn't."

She couldn't help but grin at his sulky pout.

"In that case, people say my Hecate II is plenty unfair, too. It's pretty difficult to use, though—you don't feel invincible at all. I bet it's the same way for Behemoth."

"Well, it's a problem I'd like to have. Say…what's your plan for the next BoB?"

"I'm in, of course. I've got data on pretty much all the top twenty players from last time. I'll be bringing in the Hecate this round. I'm gonna—"

She was about to say *kill them all*, but quickly changed her tone.

"—get that top prize."

Two months ago, Sinon had entered the second Bullet of Bullets, *GGO*'s battle-royale championship event, and made it through the preliminary round to the thirty-man final round. Sadly, once she was there, she only placed twenty-second.

The match started with the thirty contestants assigned to random locations, which meant a high probability of immediately being launched into a short-range battle. Sinon chose to bring an assault rifle rather than her Hecate for this reason, but she ended up being picked off by a sniper while in close combat.

In the two months since then, she'd grown much more familiar with her wild filly of a gun and also picked up a rare MP7 for practice with short-range fighting. Sinon felt she was ready to bring her giant sniper rifle to the third BoB. Her plan was simple: Find cover, wait for targets to cross her line of sight, and take them all down, one by one. She would shrug off their complaints.

Given the overload of powerful soldiers in *GGO*, she knew that if she could shoot all of them down and prove she was the best, it meant that, finally...

Kyouji's sigh of lament brought Shino back from her thoughts.

"I see..."

She blinked and looked at him. He was staring at her, his eyes narrowed as though looking into a bright light.

"You're really something, Asada. You got that incredible gun... and you pumped up your Strength to match it. It's funny, I'm the one who got you into *GGO*, and now you've left me in the dust."

"...I doubt that. You made it to the semifinals of the prelims last time, Shinkawa. It was just luck that you didn't make it through. It was too bad—if you'd gotten to the finals, you would've been in the real tournament."

"No...I didn't have what it took. Unless you've got really good luck with drops, the AGI build is at its limit. I made the wrong stat choices," he complained. She raised an eyebrow.

Kyouji's character, Spiegel, had an Agility-centric build, which was the most popular style in the early days of *GGO*.

By pumping the character's Agility as high as possible, the player enjoyed overwhelming evasive ability and firing speed— in this case, that referred not to the gun's rate of fire, but the time it took for the bullet circle to stabilize. For the first six months of *GGO*, such players reigned supreme. But as more of the map was conquered and powerful live-ammo guns were uncovered, such players lacked the Strength necessary to equip these deadly weapons. On top of that, as the guns themselves got more accurate, evasion became less helpful, and now, eight months since the start of the game, the agility build was no longer the prevailing strategy.

But still, if you got one of the powerful large-bore rifles such as the FN FAL or H&K G3 that reigned through firing speed, you could make real noise as an Agility player. The runner-up in the last BoB, Yamikaze, had an AGI build. On the other hand, the winner himself, Zexceed, played a STR-VIT balance.

But Shino was of the opinion that these stat-heavy builds only referred to a character's strength. There was another factor that was much more important.

That was the *player's* strength. The strength of will. The way that Behemoth stayed cool and calm the entire time, with enough presence of mind to put on a wry, confident grin. His source of strength was not the M134 minigun, it was that ferocious smile.

So Shino couldn't help but feel that something was wrong with what Kyouji said.

"Hmm...Sure, having a rare gun is good. But it's more like *some* of the elite players have rare weapons, but not everyone with a rare weapon is elite. In fact, about half of the thirty finalists last time just had customized store-bought guns."

"That's easy for you to say, since you've got that crazy rifle and have a good balance of Strength to use it. The difference a good gun makes is huge," he lamented, stirring his coffee float. Shino realized it was pointless to argue any further and tried to wrap up the conversation.

"Aren't you going to enter the next BoB, Shinkawa?"

"...Nope. It would just be a waste of time."

"Oh...Hmm...Well, there's school to worry about, too. You're going to a prep school for the university exams, right? How are the mock tests going?"

Kyouji hadn't been to school since summer vacation, and it

apparently caused quite some friction between him and his father.

His father ran a fairly large hospital, and despite being the second son—one of the kanji in his name meant "two"—it was expected that Kyouji would study for medical school like his brother. After an extremely tense family meeting, Kyouji was allowed to study from home and prepare for the college entrance exams in two years, thus putting him on a course to enter the medical college of his father's alma mater without losing any extra time.

"Uh…yeah," Kyouji laughed, nodding. "Don't worry, I'm keeping up with the marks I was getting while in school. No issues here, instructor."

"Very good," she joked sternly. "The amount of time you spend logged in is pretty wild. I was actually kind of worried—you're online every time I come on."

"I study during the daytime, that's all. It's all in the balance."

"With all the time you spend in-game, you must be making some pretty good cash."

"…No, not really. As an AGI-type, it's almost impossible to do solo hunts anymore…"

Shino tried to change the subject before they went down that path again. "Well, as long as you can make back the subscription fee, that's enough. Sorry, I should get going."

"Oh, right. You have to cook your own meals. I'd sure like to have a nice homemade dinner again sometime."

"Um, s-sure. Maybe later…when I'm a bit better at cooking," she replied hastily.

Shino had once invited Kyouji to her apartment and cooked dinner for the both of them. The meal itself was fun, but as they drank tea afterward, she felt Kyouji's gaze grow more ardent, which sent a panicked sweat down her back. He might be an extreme online gamer and a gun fanatic, but boys were still boys. She realized that inviting him into her home was not the smartest decision.

She didn't dislike Kyouji. Her conversations with him were some of the few moments she could actually relax in the real world. But she couldn't imagine anything more than that now. Not until she triumphed over the memories that coated the base of her heart pitch-black.

"Thanks for the drink. And...thanks for helping me. It was really cool," she said, getting to her feet. His face scrunched up and he scratched his head.

"I just wish I could help keep you safe all the time. So, um... are you sure you don't want me to escort you home from school?"

"N-no, I'm fine. I've got to be strong."

Shino smiled for him, and Kyouji looked down, as if to avoid a bright light.

She headed up the concrete stairs, which were faded to the color of watered-down ink from years of rain.

The second door was to her apartment. She pulled the key out of her skirt pocket and inserted it into the old-fashioned electronic lock. After typing her four-digit security code on the little panel, she twisted the key and felt a heavy metal thud from the latch.

Inside the chilly, dark entranceway, she shut the door behind her. Shino twisted the doorknob to get the lock beeper to sound, then muttered, "I'm home," in a flat voice. No one answered, of course.

After the wooden step with the mat on top, the narrow hallway proceeded for about ten feet. On the right was the door to her bathroom, and on the left was a tiny kitchen.

Once she'd placed the veggies and tofu from the supermarket into the refrigerator next to the sink, Shino headed into her main room in the back and heaved a sigh of relief. Using the last bit of daylight coming in through the drawn curtains, she found the switch on the wall and turned on the light.

It was not a stylish room. The cushion tiles were designed to look like wood flooring, and the curtains were plain ivory white. On the right wall was a black pipe-frame bed and beyond it a matte black writing desk. On the far wall was a small storage chest, a bookcase, and a full-sized mirror.

She dropped her school bag on the floor and took off her sand-colored muffler. Her coat went on a hanger with the muffler and into the cramped closet. Shino pulled the glossy, dark green scarf off of her nearly black school uniform and had just pulled down the zipper on her left side when she stopped and glanced at the desk.

The events after school had been wild and unpredictable, but she felt a small lump of confidence in her chest at the way she'd faced Endou's threats head-on. She'd nearly had a panic attack, but she stood her ground without running away.

That, combined with her battle in *GGO* two days ago—in which she emerged victorious from a battle with her deadliest opponent yet—had forged her courage with a hotter flame than even before.

Kyouji Shinkawa told her that Behemoth was considered invincible when working with a party. She'd seen the pressure he exhibited in person—that legend was not an exaggeration. In the midst of the battle, Sinon had nearly tasted defeat and death, but she seized her victory by force.

Maybe…

Maybe she could face her fears now, tackle those memories directly and control them.

Shino stared at the drawer of the desk, not moving.

After nearly a minute, she tossed the scarf she was still holding onto the bed and strode over to the desk with purpose.

She took a few deep breaths and drove off the fear that crawled around her backbone. Put her fingers on the handle of the third drawer. Slowly pulled it out.

Inside was a series of small boxes, of the sort for holding writing materials. As she pulled it farther out, the deepest part of the drawer was revealed. The line of boxes came to an end, and the *thing* came into sight. A small, shiny black…toy.

It was a plastic gun. But the modeling was extremely fine, and the hairline finish looked like nothing aside from real metal.

Trying to stifle the pounding that had begun just from the sight of the gun, Shino reached out for it. She hesitantly touched the grip, grabbed it, lifted it up. It was heavy in her hand. It was as cold as if it absorbed all of the chill in the room.

This model gun was not a copy of a real firearm. The grip was ergonomically curved, and the large muzzle was placed just above the trigger guard. The crude action, complete with exhaust vent, was placed up behind the grip, in what was called the bullpup style.

It was a Procyon SL, an optical gun from *Gun Gale Online*. Despite being categorized as a handgun, it featured a full-auto mode, which made it very popular as a sidearm when fighting monsters.

Sinon had the original thing in her storage room back in Glocken, but Shino had not bought this physical copy for herself. It wasn't even sold in stores.

It came a few days after she placed twenty-second in the Bullet of Bullets two months ago. Shino received an in-game message from Zaskar, the company that ran *GGO*, all in English.

Once she had figured out what it said, she found that they were giving her the choice of either an in-game prize or a real model of a Procyon SL as her reward for placing in the BoB.

She immediately made up her mind to go for the game money, having no desire for a lifelike toy gun to show up in the mail. But then she gave it a second thought.

If she was going to be sure that the drastic measures she was taking in *GGO* to heal her trauma were working, she'd have to touch an actual model gun in reality. But visiting a toy store to get one was too big of a mental hurdle. She was sure Kyouji would happily lend her one, but the potential that she might start convulsing the moment he handed it to her made her think better of that idea. Buying one online was the most realistic option, but even looking at pictures of guns on a site made her queasy and prevented her from going through with it. To say nothing of the monetary cost.

If the company behind *GGO* was going to send her a model gun for free, that solved all of her issues—and after agonizing over the decision until she was ready to burst, she decided on the real prize over the virtual one.

One week later, a heavy EMS package arrived at her door. It took another two weeks for her to work up the courage to open it.

But the reaction she had at the moment of truth betrayed her hopes. Shino shut the thing in the back of her desk drawer and consigned it to a dusty corner of her memory.

Now, Shino had finally picked up the Procyon again.

The chill of the gun snuck through her palm into her bicep, through her shoulder and into the center of her body. For being a resin model, it was unbelievably heavy. The handgun that Sinon would have spun around with her fingertips seemed to be shackled to the ground in Shino's hands.

As the warmth was sucked out of her palm, the gun began to heat up. Once it was lukewarm and clammy with her sweat, that warmth seemed to belong to someone else.

Who?

It was...*his.*

Her pulse quickened beyond the point of control, and the freezing blood raced and rushed through her entire body. Her sense of orientation faded. The floor beneath her feet tilted, lost firmness.

But Shino could not take her eyes off the dark gleam of the gun. She gazed into it at point-blank range.

Her ears rang. Eventually the sound evolved into a high-pitched scream. A scream of pure terror from a young girl.

Who was screaming?

It was...me.

Shino didn't know her father's face.

That didn't mean that she had no memory of her father in real life. It meant that, in literal terms, she had never seen her father, even in photographs or videos.

He died in a traffic accident when Shino was not yet two years old. Shino's parents were driving on an old two-lane road on the side of a mountain near the prefecture border in northeast Japan, on their way to spend the end of the year with her mother's parents. They'd left Tokyo late, and it was past eleven o'clock when it happened.

The cause of the accident was a truck making a turn that, based on the tire marks left behind, put it over the line into the other lane. The truck's driver smashed through the windshield and was essentially DOI when he hit the street.

Their compact automobile, impacted directly on the right side by the truck, went over the guardrail and down the slope, where it was stopped by two trees. Her father was unconscious from heavy injuries in the driver's seat, but had not died immediately. In the passenger seat, her mother only suffered a broken left femur. Strapped into a child seat in the back, Shino was virtually unharmed. She didn't have a single memory of this event.

Unluckily, the road was barely even used by the locals, and it was totally empty late at night. Even worse, the impact of the crash had destroyed their phone.

Early the next morning, a passing driver noticed the accident and called it in, six hours after it happened.

The entire time, Shino's mother could do nothing but watch as her husband died of internal bleeding and went cold. Something in the deepest part of her heart was irrevocably broken.

After the accident, her mother's life had essentially been rewound to before she'd met Shino's father. The two of them left their home in Tokyo and moved in with Shino's grandparents. Her mother destroyed all the remnants of her father's memory, including photographs and videos. She never talked about her memories of him again.

After that, she tried to live like a country girl, seeking only peace and tranquility. Even now, fifteen years after the accident, Shino didn't know exactly how her mother viewed her. It often seemed to be more like a little sister than anything, but fortunately for Shino, her mother never showed her anything but deep love. She remembered story time and lullabies before bed.

So in Shino's memory, her mother was always a fragile girl who was easily hurt. Naturally, as she grew older, Shino began to realize that she needed to be strong. It was her job to protect her mother.

Once, when her grandparents were out, a persistent door-to-door salesman camped out at the front door and frightened her mother. Nine years old at the time, Shino warned that she'd call the police to drive him off.

To Shino, the outside world was a place full of dangerous things that threatened her quiet life with her mother. All she knew was that it was her job to watch out for them.

So in a way, Shino felt it was inevitable that the incident happened to them. That the outside world she'd tried so hard to stay away from struck back with a vengeance.

At age eleven and in the fifth grade, Shino was not a child who played outside. She came straight home from school and read the books she borrowed from the library. Her grades were good, but she had few friends. She was extremely sensitive to interference from outside sources—she once gave a boy a bloody nose for the harmless prank of hiding her school shoes.

It happened on a Saturday afternoon right at the start of the second semester.

Shino and her mother walked to the local post office together. There were no other customers there. While her mother was producing forms at the window, Shino sat down on a bench in the lobby, legs dangling, to read the book she brought along. She didn't remember the name of the book.

She heard the door creak and looked up to see a man enter the building. He was skinny and middle-aged, dressed in grayish clothing and holding a Boston bag in one hand.

The man stopped in the entrance and looked around the office. For an instant, his eyes met Shino's. The color of his eyes struck her as strange. The whites were yellowed, and his irises were like deep black holes, restlessly moving. Now that she was older, she realized his pupils were probably in extreme dilation. Later they would learn that he'd injected himself with stimulants before entering the post office.

Before Shino had time to be suspicious, he quickly walked to the desk, where Shino's mother was conducting business at the transfer and savings window. He grabbed her right arm and tugged it, then shoved with his other hand. Her mother fell down without a sound, her eyes wide with shock.

Shino jumped to her feet, about to give the man a piece of her mind for the cruel violence he'd committed on her beloved mother.

The man put the bag on the counter and pulled out something black from within. She didn't realize it was a gun until he pointed it at the man behind the window.

A pistol—toy no, real—robbery?! The words flashed through Shino's mind.

"Fill the bag with money!" he demanded in a raspy voice. "Both hands on top of the desk! No pressing the alarm button! Nobody move!!"

He waved the gun back and forth, warning the employees in the back of the station.

Shino considered running out of the building and calling for help somehow. But she couldn't do that with her mother collapsed on the ground like that.

She hesitated long enough for the man to shout, "Put the money in the bag! Everything you've got!! Do it now!!"

The employee at the window grimaced in fear, but held out a two-inch-thick stack of bills, when—

The air in the building seemed to expand for an instant. Shino's ears throbbed, and it took some time before she realized that it was caused by a high-pitched blast. Next, something clinked quietly off the wall and rolled toward her feet. It was a narrow, golden metal tube.

She looked up again to see the employee behind the counter clutching his chest, his eyes wide with shock. There was a small red stain on his white shirt, just below the tie. No sooner had she processed this information than the employee fell backward in his chair, pulling down a cabinet of documents with him.

"I told you not to press the button!" the man screeched. The gun was trembling in his hand. A smell like fireworks reached her nose.

"Hey, you! Get over here and pack the money in!"

He pointed the gun at two female employees who were frozen in terror.

"Do it now!" he screamed, but the women just shook their heads in tight motions and did not move. They'd probably been trained on what to do in such an emergency, but no manual protected the human body against real bullets.

The man kicked the wall beneath the counter several times in irritation, then raised his arm again, preparing to shoot another person. The women screamed and ducked down.

But then he spun his body and pointed the gun into the customer area.

"Do it quick, or I'll shoot someone else! I'll do it, don't test me!!"

He was pointing at Shino's mother on the ground, her eyes staring into space without focus.

The unfolding disaster around her was overloading her mother's ability to cope. Shino instantly understood what she had to do.

I have to protect Mom.

It was that belief, that force of will that had been with her since she was a child, that drove her body to action.

She threw the book aside and leaped onto the man's right wrist—where he was carrying the gun—and bit down hard. Her sharp little baby teeth easily locked into his tendon.

"Aaah!"

He screamed in shock and tried to shake her off. Shino's body hit the side of the counter and two of her baby teeth fell out, but she didn't notice. The black gun fell out of the man's hand in the chaos. She scrambled to pick it up, all other thoughts lost.

It was heavy.

The weight of metal, pulling down on both of her little arms. The vertically lined grip was slick with the sweat of the man's palm, and his residual warmth made it feel like a living thing.

Shino was old enough to know what the tool was for. If she used it, she could stop that terrible man. Guided by this line of thought, she held up the gun the way she'd seen, putting her pointer fingers on the trigger, and pointed it at him.

He leaped onto Shino with a screech and grabbed her wrists, hoping to pull the gun right out of her hands.

Even now, she didn't know if this was a good thing or a bad thing for her. But it was plain truth that the man's grip on the gun pointed toward him actually aided her shot.

After the fact, Shino learned more than enough information about The Gun— the one the man had used in his attempted robbery.

In 1933, over ninety years ago, the Soviet Army produced a gun called the Tokarev TT-33. Eventually the Chinese copied the design as the Type 54, also known as the Black Star. That was the name of The Gun.

It used 7.62 × 25 mm tungsten bullets. This was a smaller-bore weapon than the more popular 9 mm handguns, but it had better firepower. The initial velocity of its bullets was supersonic, and the gun had the greatest penetrating power of anything its size.

This meant it had tremendous recoil, and in the early 1950s, the Soviets phased it out for the newer, more compact 9 mm Makarov.

This was not a gun that an eleven-year-old child could operate with any ability. But because the man was clutching her wrists, and Shino realized he was going to take the gun away, her fingers tensed, and automatically pulled the trigger.

An overwhelming shock ran through her hands to her elbows and shoulders, but all of the vibration that should have jolted the gun askance went straight into the man's wrists instead. The air pulsed with heat again.

He made a hiccupping sound and let go of Shino, stumbling back a few steps. A dark red circle was expanding rapidly around the stomach of his gray patterned shirt.

"Aaa…aaaaah!!"

He held his gut with both hands. She must have hit a big artery, because a stream of blood escaped through his fingers.

But the man did not collapse. Because the full metal jackets the Black Star used were powerful enough to pass through the human body instantly, they were low on stopping power.

He screamed and reached out for Shino with his bloodied hands. The blood spatter from his gunshot wound sprinkled onto her.

Her hands trembled and quaked, and she pulled the trigger again.

This time, the gun rocketed in her hands, sending a jolt of pain through her elbows and shoulders. Her whole body shot backward and hit the counter, knocking the breath from her lungs. She didn't even register the sound of the shot.

The second bullet hit the man below his right collarbone, passed through him, and hit the wall behind his back. He stumbled, slipped on his blood, and fell to the linoleum floor.

"*Gaaahh!!*"

But he did not stop moving. Bellowing with rage, he tried to push himself up.

Shino was in a state of terror. She knew if she didn't stop him for good this time, he would absolutely kill her and her mother both.

Ignoring the pain that threatened to tear her arms off her shoulders, she took two steps forward and pointed the gun right at the middle of the man's body, which he had raised eight inches off the ground.

The third shot dislocated her shoulder. This time there was nothing at all to stop the force of the recoil. Shino fell backward onto the floor. She did not let go of the gun.

The third bullet, once again shot wildly off the mark, traveled several inches higher than she aimed.

It hit the man right in the center of his face. His head struck the floor with a thud. He no longer moved or bellowed.

Shino scrambled up to ensure that the attacker was finally immobile.

I protected her.

That was her first thought. She had successfully saved her mother.

Shino looked over at the woman, still lying on the floor a few yards away. And in the eyes of her mother, the one person she loved more than any other in the world...

She saw undeniable fear directed at an undeniable target: Shino herself.

Shino looked down at her own hands, still tightly squeezed around the grip of the handgun. They were covered with dark red droplets.

Her mouth opened, and at last Shino let out a terrible wail.

"Aaaahh!!"

The shrill cry ripped its way out of her throat. Shino continued to stare at the Procyon SL in her hands. The skin from the backs of her hands to the bits between her fingers was slick and dripping with blood. She blinked several times, but it did not disappear. Drip, drip, drip, the viscous fluid fell to her feet.

Suddenly, liquid burst out of both her eyes. Her vision clouded and swam, covering the black shine of the model gun.

Within the darkness, she saw his face.

The third bullet erupted from the gun and toward his face. Even after hitting him, the mark was surprisingly small, like a little bruise. But immediately after that, a red mist burst from the back of his head. The expression and life disappeared from his face.

Somehow, just his left eye moved, that bottomless hole of a pupil staring at Shino.

Right into her eyes.

"Ah...ah..."

Her tongue covered the back of her throat, blocking her breath. As if from a distance, she felt her stomach contract violently.

Shino gritted her teeth and summoned every ounce of her concentration to throw the Procyon to the ground, then rushed toward the kitchen on unsteady feet and scrabbled at the knob to the bathroom, her palm slick with sweat.

As soon as she'd lifted the toilet lid and bent over, hot bile surged up from her stomach. She tensed and clutched, vomiting over and over until it felt like everything in her body had been expelled.

When her stomach had finally stopped contracting, Shino was completely exhausted. She lifted her left hand and hit the flush knob. With great difficulty, she got to her feet, removed her glasses, and scrubbed her hands and face over and over with the bitingly cold water from the sink.

She finished by rinsing out her mouth and drying her face with a clean towel from the cabinet. Her mental faculties were completely shut down.

With tottering footsteps, she returned to her room.

Doing her best not to look at it directly, she used the towel to cover up the model gun on the floor, then picked it up within the fabric and quickly hurled it back into the rear of the desk drawer. Once the drawer had snapped cleanly shut, she flopped face-first onto the bed, mentally and physically spent.

The droplets of water from her wet hair mingled with the tears on her cheeks and stained her blanket. Eventually she realized that she was muttering the same things over and over in a tiny voice.

"Help me...someone...help me...help me...someone..."

Her memories of the next few days after the incident were unclear.

Some adults wearing dark blue uniforms carefully, nervously

told her to give them the gun, but her fingers were too stiff for them to pry it free.

Many spinning red lights. Yellow tape waving in the wind. Blinding white light that forced her to shade her eyes. Only when she was being loaded into the police car did she recognize the pain in her right shoulder, and when she hesitantly brought it up, the officer quickly had her transferred to an ambulance.

All these things existed in her head as vague, broken fragments of memory.

In her hospital bed, two police ladies asked her about the incident over and over. She told them how much she wanted to see her mother, but it wasn't until much, much later that her wish was granted.

Shino was let out of the hospital after three days to her grandparents' home, but her mother's hospital stay lasted for over a month. The peaceful life they had before the incident never returned.

The media companies avoided reporting on the details of the case, following their own guidelines. The attempted armed robbery ended with the death of the suspected robber, with no additional public details. But it was a small rural town. The events that occurred within the post office all made it into the open—often with embellishments attached. The tale spread around the town like wildfire.

For the last year and a half of elementary school, Shino was showered with every possible derivation of the word *murderer*. By the time she reached middle school, that harassment had evolved into pure exclusion from her peers.

But to Shino, the gazes from others weren't really the problem. She had never had any interest in being part of a group, even when she was younger.

The problem was the claw marks the incident left upon her psyche. As the years passed, they showed no signs of fading. They tormented her.

Every time Shino saw something categorized as a gun, the memories of the incident flooded back into her mind, vivid and terrible, plunging her into a state of shock. Hyperventilation, paralysis, disorientation, vomiting, even fainting. These spasms could easily happen, not just from seeing simple toy guns, but even images on TV.

Because of that, Shino stopped watching virtually every kind of TV drama or movie. She suffered several fits because of educational videos in social studies class. The only relatively safe territory for her was literature—particularly the classics of old. Most of her middle school career was spent in a dusty corner of the library flipping through huge hardcover compendiums.

Once middle school was done, she begged her grandparents to let her move somewhere else to work. When that got her nowhere, she came up with a backup plan—going to a high school in the Tokyo neighborhood where Shino had lived with her parents as a baby. She wanted to be in a place without the rumors and fascinated stares, of course, but more importantly, she knew she would never recover from her trauma if she lived in that town for the rest of her life.

Naturally, Shino's symptoms were diagnosed as a typical case of PTSD, and over the last four years, she'd seen countless therapists and counselors. She took their medications obediently. But all of those doctors with their oddly similar smiles could only brush and stir the top layer of her heart, and none of them reached the place where the scars lay. As she sat in their pristine examination rooms, listening to them assure her that they understood how hard it was, she could only repeat the same refrain to herself.

You understand? Have you ever killed someone with a gun before?

At this point in time, she regretted that attitude and realized that it certainly hadn't helped her connect with them and advance her treatment. But it still formed the core of her belief. Shino's true wish was probably for them to decide once and for all if her actions were good or evil. But none of those doctors could have told her that.

No matter how badly her memories and spasms haunted her, however, she never once thought about taking her own life.

She had no regrets about pulling the trigger with the gun pointed at that man. Shino had no other choice from the moment he'd pointed it at her mother. If she was put back into that moment again, she would do the exact same thing.

But she believed that if she sought the escape of suicide, it wouldn't be fair to the man she killed.

So she had to be strong. She wanted the kind of strength that would make her actions during that incident a simple matter of course. Like a soldier who killed her enemy on the battlefield without hesitation or mercy. That was the reason she wanted to live alone.

When she graduated middle school and left her town, she said good-bye to her grandfather, her grandmother, and her mother, who still saw her as the child she was before the incident, hugging her and stroking her hair.

Shino moved to this town, where the air was dusty, the water was bad, and everything was expensive.

And that was when she met Kyouji Shinkawa and *Gun Gale Online*.

When her breathing and her pulse finally started slowing, Shino let her eyelids drift open.

Lying facedown on the bed with her left cheek on her pillow put the tall vertical mirror in her line of sight. Inside the mirror, a girl with wet hair plastered across her forehead stared back. She was slightly scrawny with huge eyes. Her nose was small, and her lips were not very full. She looked like an undernourished kitten.

She shared her body type and the short hair that framed her face with Sinon, sniper of the wastes, but nothing else was alike between them. Sinon was more like a fierce, feral mountain lion.

The first time she overcame her terror and logged in to *GGO*, she ended up dragged into an incomprehensible battle and made a startling discovery. When she was in this arid virtual world, which was nothing like the real one, she could handle any kind of gun and even shoot other players with nothing worse than a bit of tension. She didn't suffer those terrible fits.

She knew immediately that she had found the means to get past her memories. As a matter of fact, since she started playing *GGO*, she'd become able to look at pictures of guns without having the convulsions, and she was able to talk to Kyouji about the weapons in *GGO* just fine.

And that wasn't all. Shino actually *loved* the mammoth Hecate II sniper rifle she'd won half a year ago. She felt her nerves calm when she stroked the long, smooth barrel, the way that other girls her age might stroke a pet or plush animal. When she rubbed her cheek against the rounded stock, she felt its warmth.

If she continued fighting with her gun on that virtual wasteland, her wounds would eventually heal, and the fear would disappear. Thus she continued to destroy countless monsters and players with her deadly bullets.

But a voice in her heart came back to her:

Really? Is this really what you want?

Sinon was already good enough to be considered one of the top thirty players in *GGO*. She wielded an antimateriel rifle with ease—a weapon that most considered beyond any player's skill—delivering certain death to anyone caught in her scope. She was a warrior with a heart of ice, the very thing that Shino once wished she could be.

And yet in real life, Shino still couldn't hold a simple model gun.

Was it really what she wanted...?

Behind her glasses, the girl in the mirror's eyes wavered, lost and afraid.

There was no refraction to the lenses in the frames she'd been wearing since last year. They weren't a visual correction tool, but a type of armor. They were made of hardy NXT polymer, strong enough to hold firm against a bullet—according to the pamphlet. She didn't know if that was true or not, but the expensive lenses gave her a slight feeling of security, at least. She couldn't be at ease walking around without them now.

But that only meant that she was addicted to the meaningless little accessory.

She squeezed her eyes shut and felt the pitiful pleading question rise to the surface again.

Someone...help...What should I do...?

No one's going to help you!! she roared to herself, trying to drive the voice of her weakness away, and bolted upright. On the small end table next to her bed, the silver AmuSphere circle glowed.

She just didn't have enough yet. That was the only issue.

There were twenty-one gunners stronger than Sinon in that world. Once she'd bested them and sent them all to the underworld so she could reign supreme over the wasteland, only then...

Only then could Shino and Sinon merge into one, making that true strength available to her in the real world. Only then would The Man and The Gun disappear into the midst of the countless targets she'd buried, never to surface in her memory again.

Shino reached for her air-conditioning remote, turned on the heat, and stripped her uniform jacket off. She undid the hook on her skirt and pulled her legs out, then tossed it onto the floor. Last, she removed the light blue glasses and set them carefully on the edge of her desk.

She lay down on the bed and put the AmuSphere over her head, feeling for the ON switch.

A quiet electronic tone signaled that the boot-up procedure was finishing. She opened her mouth.

"Link Start."

The voice that came out was weak and ragged, like a child who had cried herself hoarse.

5

As the browser launched, it loaded up the preset URLs, spawning several layers of tabs. These were largely *Gun Gale Online*–oriented sites, particularly those that collected information on Death Gun.

He controlled a 3D mouse with his right hand, switching to the site that was most active at the moment. The banner identified it as the *Death Gun Information Repository*, with the words *Death Gun* colored in red.

The recent history showed that the site administrator hadn't uploaded any details tonight, so he moved to the message board. A number of posts had been made since he checked the site last night—a blinking NEW icon appeared here and there throughout the posting tree. He read them in order.

—*Haven't seen Zexceed or Tarako in a while. What's it been, a month? Aren't their accounts about to expire? If anyone can get in contact with them IRL, that'd be great plz*

—*I told you, no one knows. Even their own squadron members don't know their real contact info. I mean, anyone who reveals their private info on GGO is an idiot*

*   *   *

—We know the date and time that Death Gun shot them, so shouldn't we be able to look up any stories about people who died at those times to see if any of them were VRMMO players?

—Read the backlog, quit repeating the same topics. If you die while living alone, no one will notice, and we already know from experience that the police won't tell us anything. And if you try writing to Zaskar in English, they just give you their canned response about private customer information.

—I bet I know what this is. It's all a big retirement prank from Zex and Tara. You guys better come out and spill the beans before everyone stops caring anymore!

—In the end, I think someone will just have to do the research with their own eyes. Anyway, I'll be waiting outside the Central Bank of SBC Glocken at 2330 hours tomorrow night with a red rose pinned to my shirt. Come and shoot me, Death Gun.

—A hero arrives! But you need to reveal your name and address before you die so we can actually check.

—Actually, you should probably just dive in public from a net café.

—.........

He clicked his tongue in irritation and spun the mouse wheel, activating the next tab. But no matter which site or forum he visited, he did not find the precise kind of article or post that he sought.

After the second one died, the rumors wondering if Death Gun's power was real should have swept the Net, leaving every GGO player trembling in fear at the thought that they might be next, followed by waves of players deciding to give up the game for good.

But in reality, the idiots on the Net still hadn't recognized the true terror of Death Gun. They still thought it was all a big joke. The total number of active *GGO* accounts had barely taken a hit.

He hadn't counted on there being no real news coverage of the deaths of Zexceed and Usujio Tarako. Apparently there were enough unexplained deaths in the big city happening on any particular day that if there wasn't an obvious criminal angle, no single one would make the news.

Of course, *he* knew that the hearts of the two men he'd shot did stop in real life, and they had died. Because that was the power of Death Gun.

The temptation to post that information directly onto one of the message boards was overwhelming. But providing a proper source would be extremely difficult for him, and more importantly, it would diminish the Death Gun legend. He was the alpha and omega, the true absolute power in that wasteland—a grim reaper whose ability surpassed the game's management.

Well, whatever.

He sighed and calmed himself down.

The third Bullet of Bullets would begin soon. Death Gun planned to eliminate the lives of two players during the tournament, maybe three if he could manage it. Of course, he needed to get through the preliminary round without using the gun's powers, but with the twenty hours a day he spent logged in, he knew his stats were good enough.

The attention the BoB commanded was absolute. The livestream on MMO Stream attracted viewers far and wide, not just from *GGO* but from all manner of VRMMOs. Once he was both the unquestioned champion of the greatest stage *and* the people he shot disappeared from the Net, none of the fools would ever doubt the power of Death Gun again.

After the attention that would garner, he wouldn't be able to use his current account anymore, but that wasn't a problem. As long as he had the gun, it would be easy for a new Death Gun to descend upon the sands.

And he would kill more. His plans called for the number of victims to rise to seven. By then, players would be leaving in droves, and *Gun Gale Online* itself would eventually succumb to death.

Death Gun would become a legend.

It wouldn't match up to the sheer body count of the cursed *Sword Art Online*, but that was simply the act of a madman frying his players' brains with microwaves.

The power of Death Gun was much more than that. The virtual bullets he shot could stop a heart in real life. No one understood the secret of how he worked aside from him and his counterpart. Death Gun was supreme. The Black Swordsman who was rumored to have beaten *SAO* was nothing. The moment would come very soon that he took his rightful place as the greatest VRMMO player in existence.

Absolute power—legendary tyrant—supremacy—supremacy—supremacy…

He eventually noticed that he was clenching the mouse so hard, he might crush it. Slowly, he relaxed his shoulder, breathing heavily.

The day couldn't come soon enough. Once the legend was his, he had no use for this worthless world any longer. Never again would he be plagued by the asinine cretins.

He closed all of the browser tabs and opened up a local HTML file. It contained a vertical list of seven mugshots—screencaps from *GGO* cut and pasted. To the right of each picture was a name and list of weapon information. The pictures of Zexceed and Usujio Tarako at the top were dimmed out and covered with a large X the color of blood.

This was Death Gun's target list. Or put a different way, it was the number of Death Bullets loaded into his magazine. All seven of them were famous, powerful *GGO* players.

He scrolled slowly through the file until the bottom picture came front and center. It was the only female player of the seven.

The screenshot was taken from a right diagonal angle. She had short, pale blue hair tied into tufts that framed her face and covered the line of her cheek. Unfortunately, the sand-yellow muffler hid her mouth from view, but the catlike indigo eyes held a bright allure to them.

The information to the right said her name was Sinon. Her main weapon was the antimateriel sniper rifle, Ultima Ratio Hecate II.

He had seen her in person within the game many times. Shopping in the market district of Glocken, chewing on cart-sold hot dogs on a park bench, and running into battle with that enormous rifle strapped to her back. Every one of these actions was infused with a coquettish charm that stoked his desire to own her. She almost never smiled, and there was always a note of some kind of lament in her eyes, but that only increased his interest.

He was conflicted about including this Sinon girl on his target list. If she could made to be his in body and spirit, not just in the game, but in real life as well…

But his other half, Death Gun's matching arm, would want her dead. Sinon was famed throughout *GGO* as the cruel, bloodless sniper, the goddess of the underworld. No flower could be more appropriate to sacrifice to the legend of Death Gun.

He reached out and stroked the image of Sinon with a fingertip.

Within the sensation of the slick, glowing panel, he felt the softness and warmth of her body.

6

I turned on my blinker, leaned the frame sideways, and passed through the large gate.

Instantly, I felt the accusing stares of the pedestrians on either side of the tree-lined street, and abruptly slowed the motorcycle down.

In the midst of the increasing use of electric scooters, the crappy old Thai 125 cc two-stroke dirt bike I got through Agil's help made an astonishing amount of noise. Every time Suguha sat on the back, she complained that it was noisy, smelly, and uncomfortable. I tried to tease her by saying that she couldn't be like the wind if she didn't understand that sound, but secretly I wished that I had bought one of the four-stroke scooters made after the exhaust regulations kicked in.

Especially when I was riding it on the grounds of a hospital.

I puttered along the street with the speed of a donkey pulling a cart until eventually a parking garage came into view. With a sigh of relief, I drove inside and stopped the bike at the special motorcycle section in the corner, pulling out the archaic ignition key and pulling off my helmet. The chilly winter air brought a faint scent of disinfectant with it.

It was the Saturday after my high-priced-cake meeting with Kikuoka.

He sent me a message saying that the location was prepared for me to log in to *Gun Gale Online*. I made the trip with heavy heart, but was surprised to find the address was for a large municipal hospital in Chiyoda Ward.

I hardly ever had a reason to visit the city center of Tokyo, but I didn't get lost along the way. The physical rehabilitation center attached to this hospital complex was the place where I'd rebuilt my strength after escaping *SAO*.

Even after the monthlong stay there, I had to make the trip time after time for tests and other procedures. I hadn't been here in six months, but the sight of that familiar white building filled me with a strange, confusing mix of nostalgia and loneliness. I shook my head to brush off the sentiment and headed for the entrance.

The conversation I had with Asuna six days ago at the Imperial Palace nearby, where I first explained the situation, played back in my head.

"Wh-whaaat?! K-Kirito, you're...quitting ALO?!"

Asuna's wide, shocked eyes were beginning to well up, so I quickly shook my head to put her at ease.

"N-no, no! It's just for a few days! I'll convert back as soon as it's done! A-as a matter of fact...I need to go and observe this other VRMMO for a bit..."

Asuna's panic melted away, to be replaced by a skeptical look.

"Observe...? Haven't you been just making new accounts up until now? Why would you need to convert?"

"Well, it's because...of the four-eyes in the Ministry of Internal Affairs..."

With great difficulty, I explained how a large part of the reason I'd chosen the palace for our date spot was based on Seijirou Kikuoka's summons, intentionally leaving out certain details of the story.

The story finished up just as we reached the gate. We returned our tickets there and were crossing the Hirakawa Gate bridge when Asuna gave voice to her feelings, looking conflicted.

"Well, if Mr. Kikuoka's asking you, I guess you don't have a choice...but sometimes I wonder if he can really be fully trusted. I mean, I know we owe him a lot, but still..."

"I completely agree with you."

We grinned wryly at each other. The smile quickly vanished from her face, and she squeezed my hand.

"...Just come back as quickly as you can. There's only one home for us."

I nodded and looked down at the surface of the moat.

"Of course. I'll be back in ALO before you know it. I'm just doing a bit of research on what's happening inside Gun Gale Online."

...That's right.

I did not say a single word to Asuna about the true nature of Kikuoka's request—that I would be making contact with the player Death Gun, who (supposedly) wielded a mysterious power beyond the bounds of the game. I knew if I explained that, she would either stop me or demand to infiltrate the game with me.

I knew it was a selfish desire, but I had no intention of letting her anywhere near any virtual world with a hint of real danger about it.

Of course, I was sure the stories about Death Gun were 99 percent fictionalized.

A man who could kill a virtual player in real life.

At no point could I bring myself to believe it was true. The AmuSphere was nothing but an extension of the classic television set. It was easy to think of the full-dive virtual worlds as a kind of technological magic, but in reality, they were simple, useful tools—not magical items that transported the user's soul to a far-off land.

But it was that last 1 percent that had brought me here.

Several months ago, I was organizing some old digital magazines that had built up on my PC's drive, and I stumbled across a short interview with Argus's development director, Akihiko

Kayaba, just before *SAO* launched. In it, I found the following quote.

> THE NAME AINCRAD IS AN ABBREVIATION OF "AN INCARNATING RADIUS," MEANING AN ACTUALIZED WORLD. WITHIN THIS WORLD, PLAYERS WILL SEE THEIR DREAMS COME TO LIFE. SWORDS, MONSTERS, LABYRINTHS—THIS WORLD NOT ONLY BRINGS THESE SYMBOLS OF GAMING INTO REAL FORM, IT HAS THE POWER TO CHANGE THE PLAYER HIMSELF.

I had indeed changed. So had Asuna. And Agil, and Klein, and Liz, and Silica. Everyone who experienced those two years inside the game had changed to a degree that they could never be their old selves again.

But what if Kayaba's "change" was more than that...? Thanks to The Seed—the VRMMO creation package—there was now a VR Nexus made of infinitely multiplying virtual worlds. Was it possible that somewhere, in some tiny corner of the Nexus, there was some element that freely overwrote the boundary between virtual life and real life?

The automatic door buzzed open and brought a wave of heated air and disinfectant that cut through my uncollected thoughts.

In any case, if two players had died in the real world, I couldn't guarantee with absolute certainty that there was no danger in contacting Death Gun. If I admitted this to Asuna after returning to *ALO*, she would be mad, but in the end, she would understand.

She would know that as Kirito, the man who prematurely ended the Aincrad time line and unleashed The Seed upon the world, I didn't have any other choice in the matter.

After a quick stop in the restroom, I followed the instructions on the printout of Kikuoka's e-mail to reach a third-floor room in the hospital's inpatient ward. There was no patient name in the placard on the wall. I knocked on the door and opened it up.

"Hey! Good to see you again, Kirigaya!"

It was a familiar nurse I'd known while I was in rehabilitation.

The long hair beneath her nurse's cap was tied into one thick, three-strand braid with a little white ribbon waving at the end. Her tall frame, packed into the light pink nurse's uniform, created a tempting silhouette for any new patient to behold. A small name tag on her left breast read AKI.

The put-on smile she wore was as purifying and welcoming as an angel's, but I knew that she could be every bit as frightening as the situation warranted, and I wasn't fooled. After a second of paralysis and surprise, I hastily bowed.

"Ah…h-hello, it's been a while."

Nurse Aki stretched out her arms and abruptly grabbed my shoulders, squeezing my upper arms and the sides of my stomach.

"Wh-whoa!"

"Look at you, you've got some meat on those bones again. But not enough yet. Have you been eating properly?"

"I-I have, I have. But why are you here, Ms. Aki…?"

I looked around the cramped room, but she was the only one inside.

"I got the story from that government man with the glasses. He says you're doing some kind of virtual…network? Research thingy? And not even a year after you got out, you poor boy. Well, he said that since I was in charge of your physical rehab, he wanted me to monitor your condition here, so I'm off my regular shift for today. Those government agents really do have that national power to push people around—he cleared it with the chief nurse and everything. So here's to some more time together, Kirigaya!"

"Ah…i-it's a pleasure, ma'am…"

Very clever of you, knowing I can't argue back against a pretty nurse, Kikuokaaaaa, I cursed the absent agent. Instead, I was all smiles for Nurse Aki as I shook her hand.

"…So the four-eyed agent isn't here, then?"

"No, he said there was a meeting he couldn't skip. He had a message for you, though."

I took the manila envelope and pulled out a handwritten note.

> Send your report to the usual e-mail
> address. Be sure to expense all costs
> incurred, as you will be reimbursed along
> with your payment when the operation is
> complete. P.S. Don't let your hormonal urges
> get the best of you while you're alone in the
> room with that pretty young nurse.

I immediately tore the note and envelope into shreds and stuffed the pieces into my jacket pocket. If Nurse Aki happened to see that, I'd be taken to taken to a *real* court for harassment.

She blinked at me suspiciously. I answered that look with a nervous smile.

"Well, uh…Let's get connected to the Net, then…"

"Ah, of course. It's all set up for you."

She showed me to a gel bed with a number of imposing monitoring tools next to it. A brand-new silver AmuSphere hung gleaming over the headrest.

"Out of your clothes now, Kirigaya."

"P-pardon?!"

"I've got to pop the electrodes on. No use being shy—I saw it all when you were hospitalized here."

"…Is…just the top okay…?"

She thought it over for a moment, then mercifully nodded a yes. I obediently took off my jacket and long-sleeved shirt before lying down on the bed. She quickly slapped a few electrodes in various places on my upper half, to help monitor my heart activity. The AmuSphere itself had a heart rate monitor, but Kikuoka wanted to be thorough, just in case the unit itself was hacked into. That, at least, reassured me that he really was concerned about my safety.

"And that should do it…"

The nurse performed one last check of the monitoring tools

and nodded. I reached up for the AmuSphere, fitted it over my head, and turned it on.

"Okay, well...here I go. It'll probably be a four- or five-hour dive, just so you know..."

"Sure thing. I'll be watching your body very closely, so don't worry about anything back here."

"Th-thanks a lot..."

I closed my eyes at last, wondering how exactly I'd gotten myself to this position. A little ticking sound in my ears let me know the device was powered up and ready to go.

"Link Start," I commanded. Familiar beams of light covered my vision, tearing my mind free of my body.

The moment I landed in the world, something felt off.

A few seconds later, I understood why. The entire sky was yellow with a trace of pale red.

As I understood it, time inside *Gun Gale Online* was synchronized with real time. So just after one o'clock in the afternoon, the sky should have been the same shade of blue that I'd seen through the hospital window a moment ago. What was the reason for this gloomy shade of twilight, then?

After a few moments of wondering, I shrugged my shoulders to clear my head. The setting of *GGO* was the wasteland of Earth after the Last Great War. The coloring might just be an effect to add to the postapocalyptic setting.

Ahead of me was the majesty of the capital city at the center of the world of *GGO*, SBC Glocken. As befitting the king of sci-fi VRMMOs, the vibe it gave off was completely different from the fantasy cities of *ALfheim*'s Yggdrasil, atop the World Tree, and the major cities of Aincrad.

A host of metallic-looking high-rises loomed tall and dark in the sky, connected by a network of midair walkways. Colorful neon holograms were plastered in the spaces between the buildings, and increased in number closer to the ground to form a flood of color and sound.

I looked down to see that I was standing not on dirt or rock, but a street fitted with metal plating.

Behind me was a domed structure that was apparently the spawning point for newly created characters, while ahead of me was the wide main street heading into town. Weird little shops crowded the sides of the street, reminding me of the back alleys of Akihabara in real life.

The players I saw walking the street all had a distinctly dangerous air about them.

And there were, overwhelmingly, more men than women. Perhaps it was because my home game was the more female-popular *ALO*, with its world of dainty fairies, but the sight of so many imposing, well-muscled men in camo military jackets and black body armor was imposing, to say the least. Calling it *energetic* would be putting it nicely; the word I'd choose was *sweaty*. Every last one had a mean look in his eyes that said, *Don't talk to me.*

There were other reasons to be intimidated. Such as the fact that the majority of the players were carrying large, black guns over shoulder or waist.

Unlike the more decorative aspects of swords or spears, guns existed for one purpose: to be weapons. They were all designed and shaped in order to best defeat the enemy and nothing more.

It occurred to me that this was something that could be said about this entire world.

The aims of this game world were refined and distilled into three simple things: fight, kill, take. Everything that made *ALO* what it was, the idea of living another life in a world of fantasy, was stripped clean out of *GGO*.

If anything, an appearance that suggested delicacy or prettiness was only a downside. How much menace you could inflict upon the opponent in battle with appearance alone was clearly a significant variable here. Most of the men wore scruffy beards or had large, ugly facial scars to help achieve this effect.

So what did my avatar look like?

I realized that I didn't know yet, and looked down at my body.

If I was going to draw the attention of Death Gun by being an infamous badass, I'd want to look like a macho soldier out of some Hollywood action flick...

...but I had a bad premonition.

Both of my hands were pale and smooth, with shockingly slender fingers. My body, clad in black military fatigues, seemed even more fragile than my real body in places. Based on my line of sight, I didn't feel very tall, either.

As I told Asuna earlier, I hadn't created my own character from scratch for *Gun Gale Online*. If I did, who knew how long it would take for me to encounter Death Gun, who only targeted the game's most powerful players.

All of the game worlds based on the VRMMO support package known as The Seed—technically called the Cardinal system—shared just one meta-rule that applied to each and every one: the character conversion system. As long as your game was created with The Seed, you could not deactivate this feature.

By using the conversion system, a player could take a character's data from one game and transfer it to a different game run by an entirely different company. It was similar in concept to the SIM cards that allowed one to transfer their phone data to a new model from an entirely different carrier.

Let's say you had a character in Game A that had a Toughness of 100 and Speed of 80, and you wanted to transfer that character to Game B. Your strength in Game A would run through a relative value converter, which might give you a Strength of 40 and Agility of 30 in Game B. In short, an above-average muscular warrior in *ALO* would become an above-average soldier in *GGO*.

Naturally, this was not designed for copying characters. The moment an avatar was converted, the original in the old world disappeared entirely. Not just that, it was only the character that moved, not the items and equipment, so while the process was convenient, it did require some courage to go through with. In transferring "Kirito the Spriggan" from *ALO* to *GGO*, I had no choice but to dump nearly all of my items into Agil's new pawnshop storage back in Yggdrasil City. Anyone else who wasn't as lucky to know a trustworthy partner like him would have to get rid of their entire material fortune.

So the conversion process gave me a character equal in strength to Kirito in *ALO*, although given that I had started over from scratch there, I wasn't as all-powerful as the Kirito from the original *SAO*. But since I couldn't bring my appearance and items with me, I had no idea what sort of look I'd be given. Hopefully, I was blessed with a menacing soldier look, but…

I looked around the area, a bad premonition crawling up my neck, and noticed that the outer wall of the dome I'd just exited was made of reflective glass.

My eyes went wide.

"Wh-what the hell is this?!"

The person I saw in the reflection was a hundred light-years away from the look I was hoping to get.

The height was even shorter than my Spriggan form, and more slender. The hair was still black, just as before, but now it flowed smoothly from the back of my head down to my shoulder blades. Like my hands, the skin of my face was pale white, with brilliant red lips.

Although the color of my eyes was still the black of my previous character, they were much larger and shinier. In fact, framed by the long eyelashes, the innocently bewitching gaze that came back at me from the reflection was so different that I momentarily forgot it was me and looked away shyly. I straightened up and let out a long sigh.

Asuna used to tell me that the *SAO* Kirito had quite a girlish face, but this went way beyond that. I stood there, wondering how in the world I would turn myself into a menacing soldier looking like this, when a guy who had been eating something off to the side rushed up behind me.

"Oooh, miss, you're so lucky! That's an F-1300 line avatar! You hardly *ever* see that type generated. Hey, since you just started, feel like selling your account? I'll give you two mega-credits!"

"..."

I stared at him, my mind a total blank. Suddenly, an uncomfortable possibility occurred to me, and I hastily patted my chest. Fortunately, what I felt was flat and solid, and not the rounded softness I was afraid of finding. My features were feminine, but my avatar hadn't undergone a sex change in the conversion process.

In almost every VR game nowadays, players were forbidden from playing the opposite of their real-life sex. Long-term use of an avatar of the opposite sex apparently caused undeniable mental and physical effects. But because the player's sex was determined based on reading brain waves, there were very rare occasions that one was identified as the other side, and suffered quite a shock when they dove in for the first time.

Based on what we knew now, Kayaba must have already understood the ill effects of crossing those streams—at the start of the original *SAO*, gender choice was free to the player, but we were all forcibly reverted to our original state soon after being trapped inside...

I realized that I was getting lost in my own thoughts, so I concentrated on the fellow before me and shrugged.

"Uh...Sorry, I'm a dude."

Even my voice was high enough to be a reasonably alto female voice. Disappointed, I waited for his answer, but he was at a loss for words. When he found his tongue again, it was actually twice as excited as before.

"Then...you're an M-9000 series?! N-no way! I'll pay four—no, five mega-credits. Please, just sell it to me!!"

On the contrary, I'd have been happy to give it to him for free, or even exchange looks, but that was sadly not an option.

"Umm...Listen, this isn't a new character, it's a conversion. Can't sell this one for money, sorry."

"Oh...I see..."

He took one last regretful, thorough examination of my face from all angles, then recovered his spirits somewhat.

"Some people say that having a really well-used account before conversion ups your chances of snagging a rare avatar. If you don't mind me asking, how much playing time did you put into your previous game?"

"Huh? P-playing time?"

I thought it over. The total playing time for Kirito the swordsman, the account I'd taken from *SAO* to *ALO*, was at least two years long...Which would be 730 days times 24 hours...

"Let's see...ten thou..." I started answering honestly, then quickly covered it up. The VRMMO genre itself was barely three years old, so the only players who could have ten thousand hours logged were former *SAO* players, and I didn't want to reveal that about myself.

"Er, I mean, a year. It's probably just a lucky coincidence."

"Oh, I see...Well, let me know if you ever change your mind."

He took out a clear card of some kind and pushed it into my hands before reluctantly trudging off. As I stared at the card, which featured his name, gender, and guild, it began to glow and disappeared. That probably meant the information had automatically been added to my in-game data file.

Unable to get over this betrayal, I glared at my reflection in the glass. It didn't seem like there was anything I could do about it.

My conversion history was saved into my character data, so if I converted back to *ALO* I would once again be the spiky-haired Spriggan, but any time I tried to switch to *GGO*, I would still be this unidentifiable avatar somewhere between girl and boy.

Determined to live up to my motto of finding the silver lining in any cloud, I spent a few minutes until I came up with one definitive "good thing" about it.

The only reason I was in this game was to make contact with the player known as Death Gun, and observe and assess his powers for myself, hopefully not by getting shot. In order to achieve that goal, I had to garner attention by displaying my strength.

Given the type of game *GGO* was, there were doubtless very few female players, so my feminine appearance, while not what I was hoping to look like, would at least help me stand out.

I wouldn't be imposing any kind of pressure in battle, so I'd have to make up for it with skill.

As far as advertising my strength, I already had a plan for that.

It took time to make a name for yourself with standard play—conquering dungeons, or the unsavory practice of PKing. But fortunately for me, this was the very day that they were starting an event called the Bullet of Bullets, a tournament for determining the best player in *GGO*. I'd enter the tournament and jump into the battle royale. If I could hit the upper ranks and get my name out there, Death Gun would take notice—and he might even be in the tournament already.

I had no idea how well I could fight in a game I'd never played before, but there was no better alternative than trying it out. I knew that fighting with guns wasn't the same as the ranged battles with archers and mages in *ALO*, but as long as they were both VRMMOs, there would be some common ground. I'd do the very best I could—and if that wasn't good enough, the ultimate fault lay with Kikuoka for putting this ridiculous mission on my shoulders.

At any rate, first came registering for the tournament, and then came equipment.

I gave one last glance at my reflection and snorted before heading off down the main street. When I realized that I was unconsciously stroking the long hair off of my cheeks, I felt a deep gloom settle over my mind.

Within minutes, I was lost.

The strangely named SBC Glocken was made of a number of vast floors stacked atop one another. As I looked upward, it seemed to be like a compressed version of Aincrad's many floors looming overhead, with a small opening far above that admitted the sunset sky. Large buildings cut through the floors, and a variety of floating hallways, escalators, and elevators crossed here and there in beautiful disarray, but the complexity of it all was worthy of a dungeon.

I could call up a detailed map from the menu screen, of course, but it was not easy to match the location noted on the map with what I was actually seeing in real time.

In a single-player RPG, I would wander around in a daze, never to return to my original location, but this was an MMO—there was only one thing to do.

I checked out the crowd of people around me, looking for another player rather than an NPC, then trotted over and called out for help.

"Um, excuse me, could you give me directio—"

I immediately regretted my decision. The person I'd caught ended up being a girl.

Her pale blue hair was cut short in a careless style, but the fine braids tied at the sides of her forehead made for a memorable accent. Below her sharp eyebrows gleamed large, dark blue eyes with a feline hint to them, followed by a petite nose and lightly colored lips.

Wondering on the spot if this might be another misleadingly feminine avatar like mine, I made a quick inspection of the player's body, but the unzipped jacket beneath her sand-colored muffler bulged in the properly feminine ways. On top of that, she was quite small; I just didn't notice because my line of sight was lower than usual.

In a VRMMO, a good three-quarters of the time that a male player asked a female for directions, he was actually just hitting on her.

As I feared, the look on her face was of obvious suspicion—but it didn't last very long.

"...Is it your first time here? Where are you going?" she asked in a beautifully clear voice. There was a hint of a smile on her lips. I wondered what had prompted this response, then realized the answer. She was making the same mistake that the avatar buyer had just minutes ago: She thought I was a girl. Well, that was just great.

"Uh, erm..."

I nearly corrected her about my gender on the spot, but stopped myself in time.

In a way, this was the perfect situation. If I backed out here and found a male player to ask, and he mistook me for a girl as well, it would only complicate matters. My second motto was to make use of whatever I could, which in this case meant that this poor girl would have to stay under her mistaken assumption for a while.

"Yes, it's my first time playing. I need to find a cheap weapons shop and this place called the regent's office," I answered, my voice slightly lower and huskier than hers. She looked confused.

"Regent's office? Why?"

"Um…I was going to enter the battle-royale event that's coming up…"

Her large eyes blinked in surprise and went wide.

"You…just started playing today, right? There's nothing stopping you from entering, but you might not be good enough to last…"

"Oh, this isn't a brand-new character. I converted from another game."

"Ahh, I see." Her indigo eyes sparkled, and an honest smile broke across her lips this time. "Do you mind if I ask why you decided to switch to this dusty, greasy game?"

"Because…um, I've played all fantasy games until this point, and I was in the mood to try something more cyber-ish…And I'm kind of curious about what it's like to have a gunfight."

This wasn't exactly a lie. After honing my VRMMO skills on close-range sword combat for so long, I wondered how well that skill would translate to the vastly different style of *GGO*.

"I see. Well, you've got real guts to challenge the BoB right off the bat," she chuckled. "All right, I'll show you where to go. I was on my way to the regent's office too, anyway. But before that, a gun shop. What kind of firearms are you into?"

"Umm…"

I didn't have an immediate answer. As it became clear that I didn't know, she grinned once more.

"We should visit a nice big market with lots of selection, then. That'll be this way."

She spun around and took off. I hurried after the swaying muffler.

We passed through so many twisting alleys and moving walkways and stairs that I was certain I'd never be able to recall the path we took. After several minutes, we came on another wide-open street. Directly in front was a huge, flashy store that looked like a giant foreign supermarket chain.

"That's it," she said, pointing to the building as she weaved through the crowd.

The interior of the vast store was full of color, light, and sound, like an amusement park. The NPC shopkeepers were all beautiful women in revealing silver outfits flashing dazzling smiles, which made it all the more shocking to see them holding, and surrounded on all sides by, menacing dark handguns and machine guns.

"This is...quite a store," I muttered, and the girl next to me chuckled.

"It's usually easier to get the good bargains at the deeper specialty shops than these all-round stores that sell to newbies. But you can also use this place to find the type of gun you'd like, and then go do your shopping elsewhere."

Now that she mentioned it, the players milling about the establishment seemed to be wearing more colorful attire than the average, and compared to her veteran desert-colored fatigues, they came across as amateurish.

"All right. What type of build are you playing?"

I paused. Though I had converted between very different worlds, my character's general leanings should have been preserved.

"Um, mostly strength, followed by speed...I guess?"

"So you're a STR-AGI type, then. You could be a midrange fighter with a heavier assault rifle or a large-caliber machine gun as your main weapon and a handgun for your sub...Oh, but you just converted, didn't you? So you won't have much money..."

"Ah...r-right."

I waved my right hand to bring up the menu. Though I kept my statistics, I lost all my items and money in the transfer. So the number displayed at the bottom of my item storage said...

"Um, one thousand credits."

"...Exactly the starter sum."

We looked at each other and laughed nervously.

"Hmm," she murmured, putting her fingers to her chin and tilting her head in thought. "With that amount, you might only be able to get a small raygun. Or on the live-ammo side, a used revolver, perhaps...But then again, if you're interested..."

I sensed what she was about to suggest and quickly shook my head. No matter the MMO, it was never wise for a newbie to get too much assistance from a veteran player. I wasn't here to enjoy the game, but there were still rules that a gamer had to follow.

"N-no, that's all right. So...is there somewhere that I can earn a bunch of money really fast? I thought I heard there was a casino in this game..."

The girl looked troubled at this idea.

"That kind of thing is best to jump into when you've got plenty of money and expect to lose what you wager. But it's true that there are places you can gamble, big and small. In fact, even in here..."

She spun around and pointed toward the back.

"There's a game just over there, see?"

Her slender finger was pointing to a large machine, flashing with electric lights. Upon approaching it, I found that it was too big to be called a game machine—it covered the entire wall.

It had to be nearly ten feet tall and sixty feet wide. It was surrounded by a waist-high fence set into the metallic floor tiles, and an NPC dressed like an Old West gunman stood watch in the back. There was no fence at the near end, only a revolving metal bar and a square pillar that looked like a cashier box.

Behind the gunman, who regularly drew his oversized revolver from its holster to spin it on his finger and offer challenges to passersby, was a brick wall riddled with countless bulletholes. At the top of that wall was a pink neon sign reading UNTOUCHABLE!

"What's this?" I asked. She pointed out the features for me.

"It's a game where you go in the gate at the front and see how close you can get to the NPC at the back without being hit. There, see where the high score is?"

Her finger indicated a glowing red line on the floor behind the fence. It was just over two thirds down the length of the space.

"Oh…and how much do you win?"

"Well, it costs five hundred credits to play, and you get a thousand for reaching ten meters, and double that for fifteen. Oh, and if you actually touch the gunman, you win back all of the money that's been put into the game so far."

"All of it?!"

"See the carryover amount on the sign? Ten, hundred…three hundred thousand credits and change."

"That's…quite a sum."

"Yeah, well, it's impossible," she said flatly. "Once you get past the eight-meter mark, the gunman starts doing this high-speed firing pattern that's a total cheat. He's got an ultra-fast reload and three-point burst somehow, even though it's just a revolver. By the time you see the bullet line, it's already too late."

"Bullet line…"

She pulled on my sleeve and whispered into my ear, "Look, someone's going to add to the pool right now."

I tore my eyes from the gunman to see that a group of three men were approaching the game.

One of them, clad in a wintry white-and-gray camo jacket, strode up to the gate with purpose. He pressed his palm to the cashier terminal, which erupted into a bright fanfare to indicate that a transaction had taken place. Nearly a dozen people wandered up from elsewhere in the store to watch.

The NPC gunman drawled something in English that I took as a threat to "blast your ass to the moon," and put a hand to the gun in his holster. A large, green, holographic number three appeared in the air before the Arctic camo challenger, then beeped down to zero, at which point the metal bar clanked open.

"Rrraaagh!"

He roared and raced forward, then abruptly threw his legs wide to come to a stop, his eyes wide-open. He tilted his upper half to the right and lifted his left hand and leg up into the air in a truly comical stance.

Before I could wonder what kind of dance he was doing, three shining red bullets passed to the left of his head, through the space under his left arm, and below his left knee. While I'd been distracted, the gunman had fired three quick bullets in succession. The man's evasion was impressive—but it seemed as though he knew where the bullets would be fired.

"Were those...trajectories?" I murmured to the blue-haired girl, who nodded and answered:

"Yes, he evaded the bullets by watching the bullet lines."

The man in the camo took off on another mad dash when the lines of fire were gone, then stopped again, just as quickly. This time he opened his legs wider and bent over ninety degrees at the waist.

With a high-pitched whine, two bullets flew over his head and another passed through his legs. Another rush forward, another abrupt stop. It was like a game of "Red Light, Green Light."

The camo man showed considerable agility in proceeding forward seven meters. Just three more, and he'd be able to win back double what he paid to play—but that's when it all went wrong.

Until now, the NPC gunman had been firing three shots in the same pattern: pause, two shots, one shot. The man jumped to evade the last shot, but lost his balance and put a hand to the ground when he landed. By the time he recovered, it was already too late—the gunman's hand flashed, and the shot caught him on his white vest, shooting orange sparks.

The sound system played another flare, this one droopy and mocking. The gunmen swore in triumph, and the pool total on the wall behind him shot up 500 with a jingle. The Arctic camo man slumped back toward the gate.

"...See?" The girl shrugged, hiding a grin behind her muffler. "It would be one thing if you could dart left and right, but it's pretty much a straight shot forward, so you always get beat right around there."

"Hmm...I see. So it's already too late by the time you see the trajectory lines," I muttered to myself, heading for the gate.

"Oh...Hey, wait," she called out in surprise, trying to stop me. I grinned back with one cheek and put my palm against the cashier. It made an old-fashioned *cha-ching* sound.

The onlookers and the previous challenger's group both murmured in surprise, either at another foolish attempt so soon, or at seeing my appearance. The girl with the muffler had her hands on her hips, shaking her head in disapproval.

The gunman drawled a different taunt this time, followed by the same countdown.

I dropped my hips and took a dashing stance. The instant that it hit zero and the metal bar swung open, I burst forward.

Within a few steps, the gunman's hand rose and three red lines appeared from the end of his gun. They pointed at my head, right breast, and left leg.

As soon as this registered in my head, I leaped forward to the right as hard as I could. An orange bullet tracer shot past my left side. I kicked the panel on the right and returned to the center of the lane.

Naturally, this was my first experience against a gun within a VRMMO.

There were many monsters who used ranged attacks like arrows, poison projectiles, or magic spells in *ALO* and even *SAO*.

There was one way to evade these attacks. You had to read the enemy's eyes. It had to have been a sticking point with Akihiko Kayaba—every VRMMO monster run by the Cardinal system looked directly at its target when it attacked...but only if the creature actually had optical organs that could be classified as eyes.

That golden rule had to apply to the NPC gunman as well.

I focused not on the red bullet lines or the black muzzle of the gun, only on the gunman's eyes. I could sense the trajectories of his shots just from the lifeless twitching of those eyes. When they moved, I darted just enough to avoid them, left and right, up and down, weaving my way around the silent lines. Each time a bullet passed, I was already in position for the next leap forward.

I must have passed the ten-meter mark by the time he finished the second set of three, because a brief sound effect played. I barely even registered it.

The gunman released his empty cylinder, sprayed the spent cartridges behind him and popped in a full six bullets with one motion, then clicked the frame back into place within the span of half a second—cheating, indeed—then pointed it at me again.

His next attack was not the same crisp three-shot pattern. The shots came irregularly; two, one, then three. I evaded out of sheer instinct, closing another five meters. There was another brief jingle, and the gunman's lightning-quick reload.

There were only five meters left. I could see his whiskered face, twisted in what I imagined was disgust.

Beneath the ten-gallon hat, his black beady eyes swiped sideways across my chest. I determined that dodging to the side was impossible, so I flopped down and slid on the tile. The six shots flew like machine-gun fire, but I'd bought myself half of the remaining distance.

The enemy was out of bullets again. With another half a second to reload, I had enough time to reach him. But as I got to my feet, I thought I saw the gunman's eyes twinkle with pleasure.

On the spot, I changed gears and leaped as high as I could.

The air I'd previously occupied was burned through by six *lasers* that shot out of his revolver without reloading.

What the hell was that?!

I did a flip in midair and landed just in front of the gunman. Though I was tempted to drop a catchy one-liner, I didn't want to find out what other tricks he had up his sleeve—laser beams from his eyes?—so I silently slapped his leather vest instead.

There was a moment of silence, as if all the sound was sucked out of the store.

"Oh my Gaaww—!!"

The gunman screamed and put his hands on his head, then fell to his knees. A mad fanfare played overhead.

A rattling sound caused me to look up and see that the brick wall behind the gunman was crumbling outward. Before I even had time to be surprised by this, a fountain of coins was raining out, pouring over my legs and vanishing with nice little tinkling sound effects.

The big counter underneath the neon sign was dropping with eye-popping speed, and hit zero just as the waterfall of gold dried up. An awful clanging bounced off the walls of the store, then the game reset itself. The gunman was back on his feet, twirling the pistol around his finger and spouting challenges again, but after the illegal twelve-shot maneuver he just exhibited, no one in the crowd was likely to take the bait.

"...Whew."

I took a breath and left through the exit on the left-hand fence.

Suddenly, a roar of murmurs spread through the crowd, which had grown to twice its previous size. I heard people wondering who I was and what in the world I'd done.

The little blue-haired girl trotted over from the side of the crowd and stared at me with her catlike eyes. After a few seconds, she finally said something, her voice hoarse.

"...What kind of reflexes do you have...? That last one, where you were right in front of him...You dodged a laser from six feet away...From that distance, there's almost zero time lag between the bullet line and the actual bullet!"

"Umm...well..." I struggled, trying to find the right thing to say. "This thing's basically a game where you predict where the bullet prediction will be, right?"

"P-predict the prediction?!" she yelped adorably, loud enough for the entire store to hear. Everyone in the crowd simply gaped, openmouthed.

A few minutes later, once the audience had drifted off, I was in a corner of the store, examining a case of rifles.

"Hmm...I don't get this assault rifle. Why is it so big, when the caliber is smaller than a submachine gun?" I asked the nice girl, who was still helping me. She still seemed like a cat trapped between caution and curiosity, staring at me like some kind of unfamiliar creature.

"...How could you have that much evasive skill, and not even know this basic information? You said you converted, right? What kind of game was it?"

"Umm...Just, y'know, one of the fantasy kind..."

"Oh. Well, whatever. If you enter the BoB, you'll get a good look at what real combat is like. So what were you asking—why assault rifles are so small-caliber? Well, it starts with the American M16, which they designed for small, high-speed rounds that offered increased accuracy and penetration..."

She trailed off with a sour face, like she couldn't believe what she was saying. That odd reaction disappeared instantly, replaced by a gentle smile.

"...But that doesn't matter, does it? Come on, let's finish up your shopping."

"Uh...yeah, thanks," I said, nodding suspiciously. She looked away from me and began strolling past the large display case.

"You won 300K, so you should be able to afford something nice...but ultimately it all comes down to personal preference, so that's what we need to figure out first."

"Preference, huh…?"

I followed the girl, eyeing the many black and gleaming guns, but none of them stood out to me. That made sense, as I knew nothing about guns, other than that there were revolvers and automatics.

As I agonized, I eventually reached the very last one of the cases that filled the store from end to end. At this point, she ought to just pick one out for me, I thought—until something caught my eye.

In the corner of the long display case was a selection of things that looked like metal tubes, clearly not guns.

They were about an inch across and ten inches long. On one end was a metal tool that looked like a climber's carabiner, while the other end was slightly wider and featured a black hole that seemed likely to shoot something. If it was in this place, it was probably some kind of gun, but there was no grip or trigger of any kind. The only other feature was a small switch high on the side of the tube.

"Um…what are these?" I asked the girl. She looked back and shrugged her shoulders, which seemed to be a typical reaction for her.

"Oh, those are lightswords."

"L-lightswords?"

"Yes. As in swords of light. The official title is 'photon sword,' but everyone just calls them laser blades, or lightsabers, or beam sabers, or whatever they want."

"S-swords?! There are swords in this game?"

I leaned over to get a better look at the case. Now that she'd put the image in my head, they did indeed resemble the tools used by those force-wielding knights from the sci-fi movies of old.

"Sure there are, but no one actually uses them."

"Why not?"

"Because…you have to be at point-blank range to hit anyone, and you'll be pumped full of lead before you can get close enough to…"

She trailed off and stared at me, her mouth hanging open. I nearly gave her a nasty grin back, but salvaged it into a gentler, reassuring smile.

"So I just need to get close enough."

"L-look, I know you're real good at dodging, but against a full-auto rifle—ah!"

I had already turned away from her and tapped on a particular photon sword whose matte black finish I liked. When the pop-up menu appeared, I hit BUY, and an NPC employee came rushing over at top speed with a smile and a metal panel. When it dawned on me that the panel had the same green scanner that the game cashier did, I knew to put my palm on it.

It made another register sound, and the black photon sword buzzed into existence on top of the panel. I picked it up, and the employee thanked me for my purchase, then hurried back in the direction she'd come from.

"Well, no taking it back now," the girl said, giving me a look with her head tilted at forty-five degrees. "To each their own, I guess."

"Hey, if they're selling this, it must be possible to fight with it."

I gripped the short cylinder and held it out in front of me. When I clicked the switch with my thumb, it vibrated with a deep sound and a three-foot blade of purplish-blue energy crackled out of the base.

"Ooh," I murmured. I'd used my fair share of swords, but never one that was made of insubstantial light. Upon further examination, the blade was nondirectional—a narrow, circular cylinder like the handle.

I held it out at midlevel and tried the motions for the old *SAO* One-Handed Sword skill Vertical Square, which was so familiar that I didn't need the system to give me any help with it.

The blade of light growled satisfyingly as it cut a complex path in the air and came to a dead stop. Naturally, I felt no inertial resistance, as the blade weighed essentially nothing.

"Wow," the girl exclaimed with surprise, clapping her hands.

"You seem to know what you're doing. So that was a move from a fantasy world, huh? Maybe you're tougher than I gave you credit for."

"I'm not that special...This thing sure is light, though."

"Of course it is—that's about the only thing it has going for it. But assuming you're fine with using that as your main weapon, you'll still want an SMG or a handgun for your sub. You need something to keep folks from getting too close."

"...I see. I suppose you're right."

"How much do you have left?"

I checked my window and found that out of the 300,000 credits I had, only half was left. She blinked in surprise and slumped.

"Ugh, those lightswords are so expensive. Only 150K left...Since you've got to pay for ammo and armor, too, we might be limited to handguns."

"Um, I'll leave all the decisions up to you."

"You'll want a live-ammo gun for the BoB. For keeping people at bay, accuracy might be better than power. Hmm..."

She walked slowly past a case of handguns, then pointed to one.

"It'll leave you with very little, but this FN Five-Seven would be good."

Her slender finger pointed out a small automatic pistol with a smooth, rounded grip.

"Five...Seven?"

"It's the caliber—5.7 mm. That's smaller than your average 9 mm Parabellum, but the bullets are shaped like rifle rounds, which gives them an advantage with accuracy and penetration. Because they're special bullets, you can only share them with the FN P90 submachine gun, but that doesn't matter if this is the only gun you use."

"Uh, I see..."

The explanation flowed out of the pale-haired girl's mouth so naturally that it made me slightly more curious about her.

As *GGO* had fixed genders, I knew the player herself had to be female, too, but her race and age were beyond me. My instinct told me that her age wasn't that far from mine.

Of course, anyone who played an MMORPG long enough learned about the items within. Asuna and Leafa could spend minutes and minutes talking about the swords and magic in *ALO*.

But I couldn't help but feel that something was different about guns. And from what I understood, half of the guns in *GGO* were actual weapons that existed in the real world. All I could envision after hearing about these weapons was blood and slaughter. This girl around my age dove into this world enough to be a veteran player with detailed knowledge of all kinds of guns. I had to wonder what motivated her to do all of this...

"Are you listening?"

"Uh, yes, of course." I snapped back to reality. "I'll take it, then. What else should I get?"

I purchased the Five-Seven handgun she recommended, along with plenty of backup ammunition, a thick bulletproof jacket, a beltlike accessory called an anti-optical defense field generator, along with a few other odds and ends. The 300,000 credits I'd won from the bullet-dodging game were clean gone.

The photon sword on my right hip and the Five-Seven on my left tugging with an unfamiliar weight, I walked out of the store to see the sunset had turned a shade redder.

"Well, you've really been a huge help. Thank you very much," I said. She grinned behind her muffler and shook her head.

"It's fine. I didn't have any plans until the prelims begin anyway. Oh!" She stopped and checked the simple chronometer on her left wrist. "Crap, the entry deadline is at three o'clock. We might not make it to the regent's office unless we sprint..."

"Huh? You hadn't registered yet, either?"

"Nope."

Following her pale-faced lead, I checked my brand-new digital watch. The time read 14:51.

I looked up and quickly asked, "Are there any means of teleportation or something like that? Items, or spells, or special powers?!"

"I'll explain as we run!" she shouted, turning around and racing north up the street. I followed the waving muffler. Within a few seconds I had caught up, and she looked over to see that I was close before she continued.

"Here in *GGO*, there's only one method of instant travel the player can control: dying and returning to the resurrection point. The spawn point in Glocken is close to the regent's office, but you can't lose HP in town, so that's off the table…"

We ran at full speed, weaving around the NPCs and players walking the street. It was all I could do to keep up. It was already hard enough to get used to the lower vantage point than what I enjoyed in *ALO*, but she was also extremely quick. It was the absolute body control of someone who had mastered full-dive movement, not just the effect of good stats.

She checked her watch again and pointed down the street.

"The regent's office is over there. It's at the north end of the market, which is still nearly two miles away. It takes five minutes to register, so we need to get there in three minutes!"

Far away down the length of the straight main street was a giant tower glowing red with the light of the setting sun. It was a straight shot there, but even without the worry of cramping up, it would be extremely difficult to cover two miles in three minutes while avoiding pedestrians.

If I failed to make it in time for the registry period, that was my own fault for inadequate preparation, but the blue-haired girl running beside me would have easily made it if she hadn't been sidetracked helping me. I looked over, feeling guilty. She had her teeth gritted and her eyes straight ahead, full of determination. In between virtual breaths, I heard quiet words escaping her lips.

"…Please…please, be in time…"

The first round of the upcoming Bullet of Bullets tournament had to mean more to this girl than just some game event, I sensed. She had some important reason that compelled her to participate…

I looked around the area, searching desperately for some means to get her to the tower in the less than three minutes we had remaining. Immediately, a sign caught my eye.

Part of the street to our left had been expanded into a kind of parking area, featuring three small automobiles in primary colors. The panel behind them featured a glittering neon sign reading RENT-A-BUGGY! The meaning was clear.

"That's it!"

I grabbed her hand and tilted her to the side. She stammered in surprise as I practically pushed her over the shoulder of the street into the buggy rental area.

The machines were all three-wheeled cars with one in the front and two in the back. I practically tossed the girl onto the rear step of the red buggy in front and jumped into the driver's seat. The meter nearby had another fingerprint scanner like the ones I used to shop for gear, so I slapped my hand on it. It rang me up and the engine came to life.

Fortunately, the front half of the buggy worked exactly like a motorcycle did. It even operated in manual. I squeezed the handlebars and hit the throttle. The gas engine roared and the buggy shot out into the street, the front wheel floating off the ground.

"Aaah!"

A cute little scream reached my ears from behind, and two small hands grabbed me around the stomach.

"Hang on tight!" I yelled unhelpfully, then broke into a pavement-burning right turn and hit the gas. With a few shifts into higher gear, we were quickly moving at over sixty miles an hour. The overwhelming power of it finally made me glad that I'd bought that antique manual bike in the real world, rather than an electric scooter like everyone else.

I darted left and right around the futuristic four-wheel cars on the road, shifting up and down rapidly. The girl's voice hit my ear again.

"H-how is this possible?! These buggies are supposed to be so hard to drive, even the guys can barely handle them!"

Sorry, I actually fall under that category, I thought to myself, but found an excuse.

"Umm...well, I did play some racing games years ago—whoa!"

The large bus ahead of us abruptly changed lanes, forcing me to squeal the rear tires in an evasive maneuver. I dropped a gear and accelerated again to pass the bus. It was the year 2025—it made sense that very few people had experience with stick shifts anymore. Even at the driving school, the standard vehicle everyone learned on was an electric scooter. I went to the trouble of getting that midclass license with manual training because Agil's friend was giving me the motorcycle for free, but it wasn't until later that I realized pawning off the Thai-made machine on me was actually just a scheme to save him the junking fee. Some people said that it was only a few years until it was outright illegal to ride gas-engine vehicles...

I was torn out of my thoughts by sudden laughter just behind my head.

"Ha-ha-ha...Wow, this feels great!"

It took some time to recognize that the voice was coming from the cat-eyed girl. It never occurred to me that someone so tense and somehow lonely would have such a carefree laugh.

"Go, go...Go faster!" she shouted. I glared at the approaching regent's office tower, still more than half a mile away, and returned her encouragement. Head down, kicked into top gear, the engine screamed, and the speedometer said we were nearly up to 125 mph.

At that speed, we would close the distance in just a matter of seconds.

But the brief cheers of delight the girl emitted during that short period left a strong impression in my memory.

The three-wheeled buggy came sliding to a sideways stop in front of the wide stairway leading up to the regent's office.

I checked my watch: just over five minutes until three o'clock.

"We can still make it! This way!"

The girl hopped off the rear step, grabbed my hand, and started running. Her profile had already regained that sharpness that reminded me of a blade—or a high-powered gun. I tried not to waste too much brainpower wondering which of the two was her real side.

At the top of the twenty-step staircase was the unbelievably huge metal tower. It had long, streamlined curves on the front and back, with the occasional antenna disc or radar dome poking out.

"This is the regent's office, which most people call the Bridge. It's exactly on the opposite side of town from Memorial Hall, where you started," she explained, pulling me along.

"Bridge? It doesn't look like a bridge," I noted. She tilted her head.

"No, it's because it's the bridge of a ship. They call it that because it was the command center when Glocken was still a spaceship."

"A spaceship...No wonder this place is so vertical, then."

"Exactly. The SBC in the name stands for Space Battle Cruiser. Every time you enter an official event or do some kind of in game registration, it happens here," she noted. We passed through the entrance to the first floor of the Bridge.

On the inside, it was a very large, circular hall. Round pillars with detailed, futuristic designs rose up to the tall ceiling in a cross pattern. Large panel monitors lined the walls, lighting the dim interior with the color of upcoming-event advertisements and commercials for real-life companies. Most notable of all was a promotional video for the third Bullet of Bullets tournament, which was playing on the big screen dead ahead.

But I didn't have the time to stand around and stare. The girl pulled me along to the far right corner. There were several dozen tall, narrow machines along the wall. They looked a lot like the ATMs or multicontent vending machines you'd see at a convenience store.

The girl pulled me over to one of them and explained as quickly as she could.

"This is where you enter the tournament. It's just a common touch-screen machine. You know how to use them?"

"Yeah, I'll give it a shot."

"Good. I'll use the one next to you, so just ask if you need help," she said, taking her spot on the other side of the panel that separated all of the machines. I thanked her and looked down at the panel.

The home screen on the monitor said SBC GLOCKEN REGENT'S OFFICE, and to my surprise, all the menus were in Japanese. When I checked out the game's official site before diving into *GGO*, everything was in English. Fortunately, they had at least put *some* work into localization.

I poked through the menu for a few seconds until I found the Bullet of Bullets entry button and pressed it. That brought up a form asking for name, occupation, and other data. There were 180 seconds left.

The form was annoying. Why couldn't the system fill in my character name automatically? And what was my occupation, anyway? Then I noticed a small caveat at the very top.

It read: *Please enter your real name and address into this form. You may still participate with missing or falsified information, but you will be unable to receive the high-ranking prizes if you do.*

My fingers stopped still. My intention in entering this tournament was to make a name for myself and get Death Gun to target me, but my MMO instincts couldn't help but salivate at the word *prizes*. Usually that meant ultrarare gear that couldn't be won normally...

I started drifting toward the K key for *Kirigaya* before my better sense won out.

This wasn't a game excursion for pleasure. My primary duty was to make contact with the player known as Death Gun and ascertain the true nature of his powers. If Death Gun actually had some kind of supernatural power within the game, revealing any private details was unwise. There was no guarantee that

Death Gun wasn't actually involved with the game's administrators somehow, and able to access private player data.

I shook off the temptation of that rare loot and sadly left the entire form blank, hitting the SUBMIT button at the bottom.

The screen refreshed with a message saying that my entry had been accepted, along with a notice of the time for the preliminary tournament. The date was today—the time, thirty minutes from now.

"All done?" the blue-haired girl asked from next door. She had finished her entry as well. I nodded, relieved.

"Just barely. Really, I can't thank you enough for everything. Plus, I caused you plenty of trouble..."

She grinned. "It's all right. The buggy ride was fun. Anyway, what's your opening block?"

"Umm..." I looked down at the screen again. "Block F, it says. F-37."

"Oh...I see. They must have put us in F together since we registered at the same time. I'm number twenty, so that's good. We can only meet in the final."

"What do you mean, 'good'?"

"As long as you reach the final of your prelim bracket, you'll still be in the battle royale, whether you win or lose the last match. So there's a greater than zero chance we can both make it in. But if we do meet in the final, just because it's the prelims " Her catlike eyes sparkled, "Doesn't mean I'll go easy on you."

"Yeah...I get it. If we meet up, it's all-or-nothing." I smiled back, and returned the monitor to its home screen. A question occurred to me.

"For being a Western game, why is all the Japanese on this console so solid? The official site only had English on it."

"Oh, that. Zaskar, the company that runs *GGO*, is based in America, but they have some Japanese people running the JP server. From what I hear, *GGO* kind of works in a gray area both here and there, legally speaking."

"Because of the money conversion system," I followed. She smirked.

"Yep. In a way, it's like private gambling. That's why their public home page only has the bare minimum of information—not even an address. It's also why managing your character or setting up an electronic money account to transfer your credits to real funds can only be done in-game."

"It's...quite a game."

"And that's why it's kept almost entirely isolated from the real world...but because of that, it feels like my current self and my real self are two different people..."

I blinked in surprise, as a shadow seemed to briefly fall across her eyes.

"...?"

"Uh, n-nothing. Forget it. Anyway, we need to get going for the competition. It's just below us, in fact. You all ready?"

"Yes," I said, and she took me by the hand. Toward the rear of the first-floor hall, a number of elevators were lined up on the wall, and she hit the DOWN button on the rightmost one with a slender finger.

The door slid open at once and she slipped inside, then hit the B20F button. Clearly the tower extended both upward and downward from here. I felt a very real sense of dropping, which eventually slowed and stopped. The door opened.

When I saw the darkness beyond, my breath caught in my throat.

It was a circular dome, about the same size as the hall we'd just been in. The lights were as dim as possible, with most of the illumination coming from sad little arc lamps set into metal cages.

The floor, pillars, and walls were all a mesh of gleaming black metal and rusted fencing. Crude, simple tables lined the walls of the dome. A giant multiscreen holopanel hung from the ceiling. But the screens were black, displaying only the words BOB3 PRELIMINARY ROUND with a bloodred countdown, currently under twenty-eight minutes.

But what made me nervous wasn't that sight, nor the quiet strains of heavy-metal BGM playing.

It was the sensation coming from the many silhouettes lounging at the tables and leaning against the pillars that lined the outer half of the dome.

Despite being inside a video game, not a single one seemed to be excited or enjoying himself. Everyone was either whispering in small groups or sitting alone in silence. They were clearly the other participants in the BoB Prelims, and they were also clearly VRMMO veterans, hardened players with virtual marrow in their bones.

On the other hand, I probably had more sheer playing time than anyone else in this room. After all, I'd spent about two years stuck in a game without a second of interruption.

But each player had his own play style. I was almost exclusively a PvE (player vs. enemy) type, yet I could tell these grubby bastards were all tried-and-true PvPers. I could sense it from the sharp, seeking gazes sent my way from under their darkened helmets and thick hoods—they wanted every piece of information they could glean.

Since *ALO* transferred to its current administrators earlier this spring, I had essentially experienced no man-to-man combat. There was no way that much time away hadn't dulled my PvP instincts. The way I wilted under their piercing stares was proof of that.

This job is looking harder and harder by the minute, Mr. Kikuoka.

Something nudged my right elbow. I looked over to see the blue-haired girl staring at me curiously.

"…What's wrong?"

"Uh, n-nothing…" I stammered. She gave me a reassuring nod and kept her voice low.

"Let's go to the changing room. You'll want to equip the fatigues you just bought, after all."

She started walking through the midst of the players, completely at ease. There was no sign of tension in her stride. But it wasn't as if she was being ignored, either. As a matter of fact, the men around us seemed to be pouring even more antagonism on her than they were on me. One of them even menacingly expelled an empty round from the terrifying gun sitting on his knees.

She had to have nerves of steel to ignore pressure of this kind. I followed the sand-colored muffler, more surprised at her than ever.

At the back of the dome, there was a space that traded the tables for a few simple steel doors. She opened one with a blinking indicator, showed me inside, then fiddled with the control panel on the backside of the door when it closed. The lock clicked shut and the indicator turned red.

On the inside, it looked like a cramped locker room. We were the only ones in the space, of course.

"…Whew," she sighed, once she was in the middle of the room. "They're all such ditzes."

"Uh…ditzes?! You mean all those terrifying-looking people out there?!" I asked, picturing the fearsome soldiers who filled the dome. She nodded, as if it was perfectly clear who she meant.

"Of course. Showing off their main weapons a half hour before the event even begins? It's like they're asking us to work up a plan to deal with them."

"Ah…I see…"

"You should wait to equip your lightsword and Five-Seven until just before your match," she said, smiling gently. I nodded in understanding and she turned her back to me.

What she did next shocked me ten times more than what she'd said just a moment ago.

She swung her right hand to call up the main menu and hit the UNEQUIP ALL button on her equipment mannequin.

The sand-colored muffler disappeared, then the khaki jacket, the loose-fitting cargo pants, and the plain T-shirt.

All she was left wearing was a skimpy set of underwear that gleamed like some kind of multipurpose textile.

"*Wh-wha—?!*" I yelped, covering my face with my hand. Between my fingers, I saw her give me a quizzical glance.

"What are you doing? You'd better get changed."

"Er, yes, b-but…"

My mind raced, even as it grappled with by far the greatest shock it had received since the dive into *GGO* began.

There weren't many options available to me in this situation. One: I could find an excuse to escape the changing room. Two: Pretend to be a woman and just equip my body armor. But neither choice was in any way fair or honest to the girl who had given me so much help.

So I plunged headlong into option three before she could take off any more clothing and cause a true catastrophe.

My head shot down at maximum speed and I produced my namecard from the menu, then held it out to her with both hands.

"Umm…I'm sorry! I haven't introduced myself until now… Um, this is my name…man!"

"Huh? M-man?"

I felt her take the card from my fingers.

"Kiri…to. Hmm, that's an interesting name………wait………"

Because I didn't belong to any guild—known as "squadrons" here—the only other information on the card aside from my name was a sex indicator.

"Male…? What…? But, you're……"

She trailed off in confusion. Within my field of vision, which was pointed straight down at the floor, I noticed one of her cute little feet take a step back.

"No way…You're……a man? With that avatar………?"

Silence.

Unable to bear the tension that filled the locker room, I started to raise my head a tad.

The next instant, something white flashed in my face with incredible speed and exploded on my left cheek. Purple splash effects covered my eyes.

It wasn't until after I spun around like a top with the force of the impact, then slumped to the floor with little stars blinking in and out around my head, that I realized it had been the palm of her hand.

"Don't follow me."
"B-but I don't know what to do after this…"
"Don't follow me."
"B-but I don't know anyone else here…"
"Don't follow me."
I tried my best to keep up with the blue hair as she strode away, hissing back at me.

The girl had switched to a military jacket and bulletproof armor in a desert-colored scheme, with combat boots to round it out. The only thing that was the same as her in-town outfit was the muffler around her neck. As she warned me against earlier, she did not have a weapon out for show.

My equipment was similar in look, but mine was in a much darker, almost black shade—night camo, I guessed. I was prepared to abandon my usual style and go for something more ordinary, but when she told me it would take too much money to get enough styles to blend in to all of the randomly selected map types, I went with my usual fashion sense.

The very person who gave me that advice was now several feet ahead of me, determinedly not looking back. While her anger was quite justified, I also hadn't identified myself as a woman, nor had I used any specifically feminine speech. Maybe I unjustly profited from that confusion, but she also could have said something about changing clothes before she launched into it…

I shook my head to keep my thought process from getting too whiny, and stubbornly followed that waving muffler. Abruptly, she came to a stop. We had gone halfway around the dome.

I stopped as well, and she turned around to face me. Her deep blue eyes looked directly into mine. They had struck me as catlike before, but now she was more of a panther. Her tiny lips sucked in a harsh breath, and I tensed in preparation for a proper shout. What emerged was only a brisk sigh.

She thudded down into the box seat beside her and turned her head away from me. Hesitantly, I took the seat across from her.

Up on the holo-panel, the countdown to the first preliminary matches was now under ten minutes. I had no idea what to do after this. Was I supposed to move somewhere else once the countdown hit zero? Was there some extra registration step? I didn't even know where to look to find this kind of information.

I hunched my shoulders and fidgeted nervously. She shot me another look. Another deep, deep sigh.

"...I'll give you the bare minimum of information. After that, we're enemies for real," she growled. I felt the tension leave my face.

"Th-thanks."

"Don't get the wrong idea; I'm not forgiving you. Anyway, once that countdown hits zero, every entrant in here will be automatically teleported to a private battlefield with their first-round opponent."

"Ah, I see."

"The battlefield's a square arena, exactly one kilometer to each side. The terrain type, weather, and time of day are all randomized. You'll be spawned at least half the distance of the arena apart. When the battle's finished, the winner comes back here to the waiting area, while the loser is teleported to the first-floor hall. None of your gear drops at random if you lose. If you win and your next opponent has already won, the second round starts immediately. If their match isn't over, you wait. There are sixty-four players in Block F, so if you win five times, you'll be in the block championship and thus in the tournament finale. No more explanation needed or offered," she finished brusquely, though her explanation was quite helpful. The general flow of the tournament made sense to me now.

"Okay, I think I get it. Thank you," I replied.

She sent another look my way and turned to the side yet again. I could barely make out the words she said next.

"You'd better get to the final. After all the things I've taught you, I want to be able to give you the final piece of information you need."

"Final?"

"The taste of that bullet of defeat."

I had no choice but to smile. Not sarcastically or ironically, but a true smile. I couldn't help but like people with that kind of mentality.

"...Looking forward to it. Are you sure you'll be all right, though?"

She snorted. "If I actually lose in the prelims, I'll retire. This time—"

Those lapis-blue eyes cast a fierce gaze out at the sea of rivals filling the dome.

"—I'll kill every last one of them."

Those last few words had no volume to them, and reached my ears as nothing but tiny vibrations on her lips. Those lips then curled into the smile of a predator. A chill like ice that I hadn't experienced in ages ran down my back.

Clearly, she did not feel an ounce of the pressure all the men in the dome were putting on her. She was undoubtedly far more powerful than they were. She had the skill as a VRMMO player— and the underlying mentality to support it.

I held my breath and stayed quiet. The smile vanished from her face, and her eyes traveled off in thought for a moment. She waved her menu open and within seconds had produced a little card.

She slid it across the table and waited for me to pick it up before saying, "This will probably be the last time we speak like this, so I'll introduce myself here. It's the name of the one who will defeat you."

I looked down without comment. The card read *Sinon. Sex: F.*

"Sinon," I muttered, and her blue hair waved as she nodded. I tried introducing myself properly this time.

"I'm Kirito. Nice to meet you."

I extended a hand over the table without thinking, but Sinon completely ignored it and turned aside. Chastised, I retracted my hand.

After that, she said nothing.

The monitor at the top of the dome showed there were still five minutes left. Either I could sit in my chair and cross my legs, or I could try talking to her again. Approaching footsteps co-opted my decision.

I looked up to see a tall man with long silver hair hanging over his forehead coming straight for our table.

He wore an outfit of dark gray and slightly lighter gray in a camo pattern that was all right angles. Slung over his shoulder was a slightly larger gun—probably an assault rifle rather than a submachine gun. His sharp features matched up well with his slim figure. There was only a bare minimum of armor on him, and he looked very capable of traversing the battlefield with speed and agility. He gave off the air of a special forces agent rather than a hardened veteran soldier.

The man did not spare a single glance for me in the shadows, but looked directly at Sinon instead with a smile on his lips. Suddenly, those hawkish features took on a boyish roundness that surprised me.

"Hey, Sinon. You sure got here late—I was afraid you wouldn't make it."

His tone of voice was so casual and familiar that I couldn't help but wince, expecting her to hurl more of her withering vocal fire in his direction. But to my surprise, the veil of iciness that surrounded the pale-haired girl softened, and she almost seemed to smile.

"There you are, Spiegel. I got distracted by some stuff that I didn't expect to come up. Wait a minute…I thought you weren't going to compete."

The man named Spiegel smiled shyly and brushed his head with his hand in embarrassment.

"Actually, I'm here to root you on—hope you don't mind. You get to watch the matches on the big screen from here."

These two were at least friends, if not guildmates. Sinon scooted over, and Spiegel sat down right next to her without even asking.

"So what was it that distracted you?"

"Oh...Well, I was guiding that person over there around," Sinon answered, signaling me with a short, cold stare. I straightened up reluctantly and gave a brief bow to Spiegel, who had finally noticed my presence.

"Hi, I'm 'that person.'"

"Oh, er...nice to meet you. Are you a...friend of Sinon's?"

Spiegel had an air about him, to be sure, but he turned out to be more courteous than his appearance suggested. Either that, or he was also confusing my gender.

I was figuring out which answer would be the most entertaining when Sinon cut off my fun.

"Don't be fooled. He's a man."

"Huh?"

Spiegel went wide-eyed. I had no choice but to introduce myself normally.

"Uh, I'm Kirito. Male."

"M-male...Which, um...means you're, uh..."

He still looked confused. Sinon and I shared a glance. It looked like he was having trouble processing the fact that Sinon had been working with another male player.

Intrigued by this reaction, I decided to toss a little fuel onto the fire.

"Actually, I've got a lot to thank Sinon for, in a variety of ways."

Sinon turned her blue lasers on me and growled through pursed lips. "I...I haven't done any such thing. And you're in no position to call me by name..."

"What's with the cold shoulder all of a sudden?"

"Cold?! We're complete strangers!"

"Even though you helped me coordinate my outfit?"

"Th...that was because I thought you were—"

Suddenly, our bickering was interrupted by the quiet BGM in the dome fading away, to be replaced by a blaring electric guitar lead. Next, a soft, electronically generated voice boomed over the heads of the hundreds in attendance.

"Thank you for your patience. The preliminary blocks of the third Bullet of Bullets tournament will now begin. All players registered will be automatically teleported to the first-round field map at the end of the countdown. Best of luck."

A great cheer chose from the room. The rattle of automatic fire and the screech of lasers followed, the various types of gunfire shooting up to the ceiling like fireworks. Sinon quietly got to her feet and jabbed a finger at me.

"You'd better make it to the final. I need to blow your head off."

I rose in turn and grinned. "Well, I was never one to turn down an invitation to a date."

"Wh-why, you..."

The twenty remaining seconds of the countdown trickling away, I waved to Sinon and faced forward in preparation for the teleport. As I did so, I met Spiegel's gaze.

When I saw the wariness and hostility in his eyes, I was briefly struck by the idea that I'd gone too far, and its accompanying regret.

But the next moment, my body was surrounded by a pillar of blue light that flooded my vision.

When I could see again, I was atop a hexagonal panel floating in the midst of darkness.

There was a pale, red holo-window in front of me that loudly proclaimed *Kirito vs. Uemaru*. Unlike *SAO*, in which all players had to spell their names in the Western alphabet, *GGO* allowed proper Japanese characters, so his name was spelled in actual kanji. I didn't recognize the name, of course. At the bottom of the window it said, *Preparation time: 58 secs. Field: Lost Ancient Temple.*

I interpreted the minute of prep time to be meant for optimizing equipment for the chosen map, but that meant nothing to me without any backup gear or knowledge of *GGO*'s terrain. I called up the menu and switched to my equipment window—which resembled that of *ALO*'s—and set the Kagemitsu G4 lightsword as my main weapon, and the Five-Seven as my sidearm. Once I'd ensured that none of my armor was forgotten, I closed the window.

As the remaining time slowly counted down, a sudden possibility struck my brain.

That ferocious smile I'd seen Sinon wear for just a moment. It was like pure, distilled lethality, a rifle bolt that could pierce any armor or shield.

Her voice sounded inside my head so clearly that it could have been telepathy.

This time, I'll kill every last one of them, she'd said. The words were trite, even childish, but they succeeded in delivering that familiar chill I'd experienced so many times since the *SAO* days that I couldn't count. It was as if real, tangible will, transcending any kind of in-game role-playing, was radiating out from her tiny body.

I'd met few players who could make me feel that sort of willpower within the virtual realm. And as far as female players went, the only one who had reached this level was Asuna, and at her most extreme. Actually, even Asuna the Flash, previously known as the Mad Warrior, had never given off such a fierce energy.

Was it possible? Could this blue-haired girl in fact be the very Death Gun I was seeking?

The ugly, metallic rasp of Death Gun's voice in the recording that Kikuoka played for me was completely unlike Sinon's pure, crisp tones. But unlike *SAO*, *GGO* was a normal game. A single player could easily have multiple characters that she could switch between at the log-in screen.

Plus, based on what she said, Sinon had absolute confidence in her ability to reach the Bullet of Bullets final. If my expectation that Death Gun would be there was correct, that lowered my list of potential candidates to thirty. Sinon would be one of them.

In all honesty, I did not want to consider that possibility. She had showed me to the shop and walked me through many facets of the game, and I never got a hint of murder from her personality. If anything, there was a sad loneliness about her.

So which was the real Sinon?

No use thinking about it now. Once we trade sword blows—er, gunshots—I might understand more.

I raised my eyes at the exact moment the countdown hit zero. The teleportation effect surrounded me again.

The next thing I saw was a gloomy sunset.

Wind blew past, a high-pitched whistling in my ears. Scraps of yellow cloud floated by overhead, and dried grass rustled fiercely at my feet.

Right nearby was a massive stone column, though I couldn't have identified Ionian style from Corinthian. It was part of a pattern, a layout of columns in a three-sided square shape, each one about three yards from the next. Some of them had withered away at the top, and some were completely collapsed. It looked just like some ancient temple that had fallen into ruin ages ago.

Out of instinct, I scrambled to the nearest column and scanned the surroundings.

The faded grasses continued in all directions, and beyond the low hill I could see a number of other ruins like the one I stood in now. From what Sinon said, the maps were a thousand meters on each side, but it was clearly several dozen times that distance to the horizon. There must have been rivers or cliffs at the boundaries to prevent moving beyond the map.

I remembered more of her explanation. The contestants were placed at least half of the full distance apart, but I didn't see anyone. My opponent must have been hiding behind cover like me. There were no cursors to indicate enemy location, so I had to start by finding my foe.

I could choose to hide until the other guy got tired of waiting and needed to act, but waiting wasn't my style. It seemed liked a better idea to sprint to the nearest ruins in the hope of drawing fire so that I could discern the enemy's location. I brushed the Five-Seven on my waist with my left hand.

At that moment, a stronger breeze brushed past, snapping the nearby grass back and forth. Once the gust had passed, at the exact moment that the grass stood back up, a silhouette abruptly and silently got to its feet barely twenty yards away.

He had an assault rifle in both hands, trained right on me. The image instantly burned into my mind through my retinas: brown stubble pressed up to the barrel, goggles covering the upper half of his face, and a helmet topped with dummy grass. We were the only two people on the map, so this had to be Uemaru.

I had no idea how he'd approached so quickly. Clearly, a big part of the reason was the camo he was wearing. It was colored the exact same khaki as the grass around us, in a fine, vertical-striped pattern. That was an example of the sixty-second preparation period being put to good use.

Dozens of red lines shot out of the black rifle on the enemy's shoulder, bullet lines that showed where his shots would land, crossing entirely over me and the space around me.

"Whoa!" I shrieked, jumping on instinct. That took me in the direction of the least dense number of bullet lines—directly upward.

Katatatata! His rifle cracked loudly, and I felt two hard impacts on my right shin. The HP bar that was fixed in the upper left corner of my vision dropped about 10 percent. There were too many bullets to dodge them all—I belatedly remembered Sinon's warning about full-auto fire.

I did a flip in midair and landed atop the broken column behind me, pulling the Five-Seven out of its holster and preparing to shoot back.

But Uemaru didn't give me the time to get ready. More of the countless red lines intersected my chest.

"Aaaah!"

I wailed pitifully and fell backward off the pillar, but another of the bullets grazed my left arm, tearing away more HP.

Most of the hail of gunfire hit the stone column, sending little shards flying. I held my limbs close, trying to keep my body safely hidden in the shadow of the pillar.

This is nothing at all like a sword-on-sword battle!

The bullet-dodging game I played with the NPC gunman featured a six-shooter with intervals in between, which required all of my nerves to conquer. But this level of bullet hell—over ten shots a second—was beyond my ability.

If I was going to use that Kagemitsu to chop off Uemaru's ugly whiskers, I needed to get right up in his face, but at this rate I would be riddled full of holes far before I got anywhere near him.

Since full evasion was impossible, I'd have to defend against the bullets somehow. Sadly, this world only had defensive fields that neutralized lasers, and no magical shields that could stop a live round. Even in *SAO*, I could have used my sword as a shield using the Weapon Defense skill.

I put my hand to the lightsword, still hooked to my belt by the carabiner. If only I could deflect some of the bullets with the sword. It shouldn't be impossible—they did that in those old sci-fi movies about the wars among the stars. Since this game was made in America, they had to have considered the possibility. But if I was going to pull off such a maneuver, I'd need to accurately predict the trajectories of the incoming bullets…

No, wait.

That was possible. After all, what were the bullet lines for, if not seeing where the gunfire was going to be?

I swallowed and pulled the sword off of my belt.

The shots had stopped for the moment. If I had to guess, Uemaru had shrunk back down into the grass so he could flank me, either to the left or the right.

I closed my eyes and let my ears take over.

The wind was still blowing noisily. I shut the howling sound effects out of my mind. Next, I focused on the rustling of the dried-out plants around me. Amid the regular waving pattern of the sound, I searched for anything irregular.

Being able to tell apart the different sound effects in a VR space was a considerable technique, a system-independent skill that served me well in *SAO*. I would never have been able to hunt down the S-rank Ragout Rabbit without being able to discern fine differences in sound.

What about now?

I detected an irregular noise moving slowly from my seven to my nine. It moved for two or three seconds, then stopped, testing my reaction.

The enemy resumed moving, then stopped, then starting moving again.

"Go!" I screamed, launching myself directly at his hiding spot.

Uemaru clearly wasn't expecting me to charge straight for the place where he was crawling on all fours. He got up to his knees from the dead grass and pulled his rifle up to a shooting position, but that action took him a second and a half.

By that point, I had already closed half of the eighty feet between us. I clicked the switch of the photon sword in my hand as I ran. With a satisfying *vumm*, it produced a bluish-purple glowing blade.

For the third time, Uemaru's assault rifle showed a dozen or more bullet lines. I'd been evading on instinct alone before, but this time I kept my eyes forward. Ignoring the prickling of fear in my neck, I noted that all of the lines did not appear at the same time—there was a slight time lag between them. That was an indication of the order the bullets were fired from the rifle muzzle.

Out of all of the bullets, only six of them were currently due to intersect with my body, which was quite a bit smaller than my real one. The rest were going to miss slightly to the sides, or above and below. Based on the fact that we were actually quite close, this level of accuracy told me that either the enemy's gun or his personal skill were, in fact, not very precise.

That familiar sense of tension that every PvP battle featured told me that my own gears had finally shifted into battle mode. It was that familiar sense of acceleration: edges of my vision stretched out, target in the center much clearer than before. As time slowed down around me, my mind seemed to speed along much faster.

The enemy's rifle flashed orange. In that instant, my light-sword perfectly caught the first two of the six bullets that would hit me.

Bzz, bzap! Orange sparks flew from the surface of the glowing sword. By the time I even processed that reaction, my right arm was already flashing like lightning, holding the photon sword over the line that connected the third and fourth bullet trajectories. Once again, the bullets were knocked aside by the high-density energy blade.

It took a lot of concentration to keep charging while the bullets that *weren't* meant to hit screamed past my ears, but I gritted my teeth and kept swinging away.

Five…then six! Having successfully deflected all of the accurate shots, I redoubled my speed to close the remaining distance.

"N-no way, man!"

Uemaru's heavily bearded chin dropped in shock. But his hands didn't stop moving. He released the empty magazine with comfortable ease, pulled a spare from his waist, and moved to pop it in.

I pointed the Five-Seven at him, hoping to prevent him from finishing the reload. The instant I touched the trigger, I was surprised to see a pale green circle over the enemy's chest, but I pulled it five times in quick succession anyway.

The recoil in my elbow and shoulder was much lighter than I expected, and two of the shots landed on Uemaru's shoulder and side within the transparent circle. The other three disappeared into the grass behind him, but the two that hit must have broken through his armor to do damage. The HP gauge in the upper right lost a bit of ground. Uemaru stumbled and stopped for just a moment.

That was all I needed.

The instant I was within sword range, I twisted myself to the right—

And launched myself off the virtual ground with all the added velocity of my sprint, slamming the enemy directly in the chest with what would have been called a Vorpal Strike back in *SAO*.

The blade of light easily sank into his chest up to the hilt, roaring and rattling like a jet engine. For an instant, I felt all of that energy squirming around in his body without an outlet.

The next moment, a cone of ferocious light and sound erupted from my right hand, and the enemy's body turned into countless tiny polygons, expanding into nothingness.

I slowly got to my feet, feeling the lasting numbness of battle in every inch of my body. Out of habit, I waved the lightsword back and forth and nearly stashed it over my back until I came to my senses and quickly shut it off.

Only when the sword hilt was clicked onto the snap ring on my waist and the handgun was back in its holster could I let out the breath I'd been holding. Up in the evening sky, a giant message of congratulations was displayed over the hanging clouds.

Somehow, I'd won my first-round match. The fact that I could defend against the bullets with my lightsword was a very good sign. But that kind of high-speed sword work required phenomenal concentration, and I could feel my nerves popping and smoking.

Four more of these exhausting battles?

I slumped my shoulders as the blue teleportation effect swallowed my body. The lonely whistling of the wind died away, to eventually be replaced by the bustling noise of the crowded waiting area.

Apparently I had been teleported back to the same box seat against the wall. I looked left and right, but neither Sinon nor Spiegel was present. Sinon was probably still in a battle, but I couldn't help but be curious where her male acquaintance had gone. I eventually spotted a familiar-looking urban camo closer to the center of the dome. He hadn't noticed my return, and was watching the monitor hanging from the ceiling with great interest.

I looked up to see that the giant screen, which had previously been running the pretournament countdown, was now displaying a number of battles at once. They were showing off players blasting rifles and pistols in desert, jungle and ruin settings with all the style and impact of an action movie.

Most likely, these were only the ongoing battle scenes out of the hundreds of matches happening concurrently. When the occasional player took too much fire and burst into pieces, the crowd watching from the floor gave a great cheer.

I took a few steps forward, hoping to see if I could get a glimpse of Sinon in action. I started checking each one in order from the upper left corner, but the camera work was so frantic that it was nearly impossible to tell them apart. It seemed like a better idea to concentrate on finding her distinguishing light blue hair.

Which is why my heart nearly stopped when someone abruptly spoke into my right ear. It was as if the low, raspy, metallic voice was bypassing my eardrum to go straight to the sensory center of my brain.

"Are you, the real thing?"

"…?!"

I jumped back and turned around out of sheer instinct.

The first thought that crossed my mind was *Ghost*.

Not a real ghost, of course. Around the sixty-fifth floor of Aincrad, which was themed after old castle ruins, there were common ghost-type enemies. They were covered with tattered dark gray cloaks, the hoods pulled low over absolute darkness except for faintly glowing red eyes.

The person standing before me in the dim light of the dome was extremely similar in appearance to those ghosts. My unconscious reaction was to leap backward and draw my sword. The urge was so strong that I couldn't prevent my hand from twitching.

With a faint grunt, I looked down at his feet. Through the scraps of the ripped cloak, I could barely make out the tips of faded, grungy boots.

This was a player, not a ghost. Recognizing that obvious fact, I let out a slow breath. Upon closer examination, the red eyes weren't little glowing hellfires, but simply lenses within the black goggles that covered his entire face. Irritated at both my amateur reaction and his lack of manners in accosting another player at point-blank range, I didn't feel in the mood to be polite.

"What do you mean, 'real thing'? Who are you?"

But the gray-cloaked player did not name himself, and took another step forward to close the distance again. I didn't back away this time, staring right back at the robotic gaze from just eight inches away.

His unpleasant voice, obviously affected by some kind of voice modulator, rasped again.

"I saw, your match. You used, a sword."

"Y...yeah. It's not against the rules," I replied. The AmuSphere unhelpfully re-created the unease I was feeling, causing my voice to crack. The gray cloak approached even closer, as if recognizing that weakness.

The next statement came so quietly that I could barely hear it without concentrating, even at that distance.

"I'll ask, again. Are you, the real thing?"

Before I even had time to process and understand his question, a bolt of lightning struck my brain out of the blue, stopping me still.

I know him!!

I was sure of it. I had met him somewhere before. We had come face-to-face and exchanged words.

But where? The only people I'd spoken to since logging in to *GGO* were the avatar buyer right at the spawning point, Sinon during her assistance with my shopping and registration, and her friend Spiegel. So it wasn't in *this* world.

ALO, then? Did I meet him back in *Alfheim*, while we both had different avatars? I frantically consulted my memory index, trying to match the style of speech and general air to anyone I knew. But nothing turned up. I couldn't remember meeting anyone with such a chilling presence.

Where? Where have I met him before…?

The tattered cloak waved, and a thin arm extended from the middle. I nearly jumped backward again, but the hand, clad in a similarly ragged glove, was empty.

The empty hand called up a menu window where I could see, its movements dull and lifeless. The screen showed a tournament field with six blocks—the current bracket of the third Bullet of Bullets.

His needle-like finger tapped at Block F, which expanded to fill the screen. He clicked again, and it zoomed into the center of the block.

My gaze was drawn to the spot his finger indicated.

There were two names: UEMARU on the left and KIRITO on the right. A glowing line extended from my name on the right. It had already been officially announced that I beat Uemaru and advanced to the second round.

The finger moved slightly, tracing the name KIRITO from top to bottom. He spoke again.

"This, name. That, attack. Are you, the real thing?"

A moment later, I was struck by my third great shock.

My knees trembled and nearly buckled, but I held my poise just in time.

This guy knows me!

He knew the source of the name Kirito, and the sword skill that I used to defeat Uemaru as well.

Meaning...I hadn't met him in *GGO* or in *ALO*.

SAO. Sword Art Online. Somewhere in the floating castle Aincrad, the setting of that game of death, I had met this man.

Whatever avatar was behind that tattered, creepy mask—no, *whoever* was on the other side of that *avatar,* lying down, connected to an AmuSphere—they were an *SAO* Survivor, just like me.

My pulse was ringing like an alarm bell. If it wasn't for the gloom of the dim room, it would have been quite apparent that I was white as a sheet.

Calm down, just calm down, I repeated to myself, over and over.

There was no need to panic just because I'd met another survivor of *SAO.* Not long before the collapse of Aincrad, there were plenty of articles and stories being shared about my Dual Blades extra skill, and my public duel with Heathcliff of the Knights of the Blood. And the Vorpal Strike I'd just used on Uemaru was a very commonly used One-Handed Sword skill. Any player of a decent level in Aincrad could have put two and two together after watching the footage and checking the tournament bracket. I probably would have tried the same thing if I recognized an old acquaintance from those days here in the dome.

So there was no reason to be afraid. There *shouldn't* have been.

Then why was I so...

For an instant, just as he removed the bracket and was pulling his thin arm back into his cloak, my eyes caught sight of something.

On the inside of his wrist, just above the glove that looked more like ragged bandages wrapped around his hand, there was a glimpse of pale white skin. And, clear as day, a tattoo about two inches across.

The design was a caricature of a Western-style coffin. On the lid was an eerie, leering smile. That lid was lifted slightly off the hinges so that a white skeletal arm extended out from the darkness within, beckoning the viewer closer. It was the exact same mark that I'd seen on the arm of a man who paralyzed me with poisoned water and tried to kill me.

A coffin, grinning.

It was practically a miracle that I successfully avoided screaming, falling to the floor, or getting auto–logged out because of some kind of brain-wave trauma. Instead, I showed no reaction.

The red, glowing goggles stared through me. Eventually, the player in the tattered cloak rasped again.

"Did you, not understand, the question?"

I slowly and deliberately nodded my head.

"…Yes. I don't understand. What do you mean, the real thing?"

"…"

The gray cloak took a silent step backward. The red gaze flickered once, as if he blinked. After several extremely long seconds, his voice was even more robotic than before.

"…In that case, fine. But, if you are, a fake using the name…or, the real thing…"

He finished his sentence as he was turning away.

"…*I will, kill you.*"

It did not strike me as a harmless bit of in-game role-playing.

The tattered cloak disappeared into the crowd without a sound, just like an actual ghost. There were no lingering signs that any player had been there just seconds ago.

This time I really did stagger, barely keeping my balance, and stumbled over to the nearby box seat. I hugged my slender legs and pressed my forehead against my knees.

When I closed my eyes, I saw that tattoo again, bright and clear, even though it had only caught my eye for a fraction of a second.

There was only one group in Aincrad who used that symbol as their identifier.

The murderous red guild, Laughing Coffin.

* * *

Over the course of those two long years trapped in *SAO*, it wasn't long until the emergence of "orange" players, criminals who took out their frustrations by stealing money and items from other players. But those actions took place within certain bounds—usually a big group surrounding a few helpless victims and forcing them to trade, or perhaps using a paralysis venom.

Since obliterating one's HP bar with a direct attack would cause the player to die in real life, no one had the guts to go through with that. These were ten thousand people severely addicted to online games—not the type of people who went around committing violent crimes in regular life.

It was the existence of one single player with a very different mentality that broke the unwritten rule not to take every last HP.

The man's name was spelled PoH but pronounced "pooh." It was a silly-sounding name, but despite that—or perhaps because of it—his presence commanded attention wherever he went.

The biggest reason for this was PoH's exotic looks and his multilingual status—he seemed to be half-Japanese and half-Western. His Japanese was peppered with smooth, fluent English and Spanish slang, which made him sound like a cool pro DJ rapping at the table. It was easy for him to bring others around to his way of thinking, turning simple MMO gamers into cooler, tougher outlaws than they'd ever been, and he, in life.

The second reason for his charismatic nature was PoH's outright strength.

His skill with the dagger was nothing short of genius. The blade flashed like an extension of his hand, and he attacked monsters and players alike without needing to rely on the system's built-in sword skills. In the later stages of the game, once he'd found a terrifying dagger by the name of Mate-Chopper, he was a menacing enough force to unnerve even the front-line players.

PoH's leadership skills were on the same level as Heathcliff's, but in the polar opposite direction. Very gradually, over time, he began to remove many of the mental roadblocks that kept his followers within certain bounds.

A year after the game's start, on New Year's Eve, 2023, PoH's gang of nearly thirty players attacked a small guild that was enjoying an outdoor party at one of the map's sightseeing spots, and killed all of them.

The next day, the various information dealers around Aincrad were trumpeting the formation of Laughing Coffin, the first unofficial "red" guild in the game.

At the very least, I knew the gray-cloaked man who made contact was not PoH. His flat, broken speech was nothing in the least like PoH's machine-gun staccato.

But I couldn't help but feel that I knew someone in Laughing Coffin who spoke this way. I must have come face-to-face with him and traded words, if not sword strikes. Not a rank-and-file soldier, but a very high-ranking officer. How could I guess all of these things, yet not remember his face or name?

But in fact, I knew why—my own mind was refusing to remember.

Laughing Coffin was formed on January 1, 2024, and obliterated on a summer night eight months later.

It was not a spontaneous breakup, or the result of infighting. A large-scale raid party of over fifty of the game's best front-line fighters put them to the sword.

This method could easily have been taken much earlier. The reason it didn't happen for eight months was because Laughing Coffin's hideout took that long to pin down.

Any houses or apartments available for players to buy in Aincrad, whether in a town or outside in the wilderness, could be easily and accurately located with an NPC real estate agent. We assumed that a place that could house thirty would need to be a mansion or fortress, so information dealers hired by the group began crosschecking all of the large-scale residences starting from the first floor and going up.

Although this did turn up the bases of several smaller orange guilds, after several months there was still no sign of the crucial Laughing Coffin hideout.

And there was good reason for that—they were actually using an already-cleared minor dungeon on a lower floor as their base of operations, crammed into the safe haven zone within. It was just a little cave, the kind of location the game designers would have set up and then forgotten completely. The powerful front-line players only bothered with the labyrinth towers that led to the next floor, and the midlevel types preferred the larger dungeons with more players around. Of course, one had to assume that a few unlucky souls coincidentally ran across that tiny cave, and it was all too easy to imagine how they were prevented from telling the tale.

The suspected reason that Laughing Coffin's base was finally identified after eight long months was that one of their members gave in to his guilty conscience and revealed the location to another player. A reconnaissance mission determined that it was indeed the cave in question, which led to the formation of the massive raid party. The leader was an officer from the Divine Dragon Alliance, the largest guild in the game. Several other principal members from the Knights of the Blood and other guilds were present, and even I participated as a solo.

The assault on their base happened at three in the morning.

Our numbers and levels were significantly higher than those of Laughing Coffin. We assumed it would be quite easy to seal off the ways out of the safe haven area and force them to surrender without bloodshed.

But just as someone from their group had informed on the location of their hideout, they learned about our top secret plan through some means still unknown.

When we charged into the dungeon, not a single member of Laughing Coffin was in the safe zone. But they had not fled ahead of time. They were all hiding in the dungeon's offshoot branches, and attacked us from behind once we were inside.

They used traps, poison, blinding—every kind of sabotage they could attempt. Though the raid party was thrown into chaos at first, responding appropriately to unexpected circumstances was one of the most crucial qualities to the game's best players. The raid regrouped quickly and led a furious counterattack.

But there was one unforeseen difference between Laughing Coffin and the raid party.

It was the resistance to the idea of killing. When we realized that the insane members of LC were not going to surrender, even when reduced to slivers of HP, our group was rattled.

We had discussed this possibility before the operation. The consensus was that we would not hesitate to wipe out the enemy's HP entirely if that was necessary. But it might have been the case that none of our entire raid, including myself, truly had what it took to deliver that final blow, knowing the enemy's HP was down in the red. Some of us even threw our swords aside and took a knee.

We were the first to lose a few members to the raid. When the front-line team fought back with rage and grief, several from Laughing Coffin died.

After that, it was bloodstained hell.

When the battle was over, the raid party was short eleven, while Laughing Coffin had lost twenty-one. Two of those had been at my hand.

Among the names of the dead and captured, we did not find PoH, their leader.

If the player in the tattered gray cloak was one of the twelve Laughing Coffin survivors who was sent to the prison in Black-iron Palace, then we must have had a conversation after the battle. If I could remember his style of speaking, but not his face or name, that was because I was actively trying to forget everything about that battle.

…No.

What if the man under that cloak was one of the two I killed?

I shook my head violently, still clutching my knees on top of the chair. I clenched my teeth so hard they could have broken, and lashed my mind back into shape.

The dead did not come back to life. The four thousand victims of the *SAO* Incident, whether I loved or hated them, would never come back. So the cloaked man had to be one of the twelve survivors of Laughing Coffin. And I knew all of those names. I grimaced against the pain, trying to dig deep, deep into that terrible memory...

Then I gasped, realizing another possibility.

The twisted, metallic voice—it was only a rasping whisper, but what would it sound like if shouted at full volume?

The scream on the audio file I heard a week ago came back to echo in my ears.

This is the true power, the true strength! Carve this name and the terror it commands into your hearts, you fools! My name, and the name of my weapon, is...Death Gun!!

It was the same. The exact same. The voice was identical.

Was the man in the gray cloak...Death Gun?

If that was true, then I had already completed my duty: to attract attention in *GGO* and find myself targeted by Death Gun.

But...I couldn't have imagined that I would learn *this* fact— that Death Gun was a survivor of *SAO*, and a member of the murderous Laughing Coffin, to boot.

A man who had possibly killed two players in real life with gunshots from within the game. What if that power...was real...?

I nearly screamed when someone suddenly clapped a hand on my shoulder. I flinched and looked up to see pale blue hair.

"...You look like you've seen a ghost," Sinon said, frowning. Somehow I managed to work my cheeks into a smile.

"Uh...n-no, it's nothing..."

"Was it really that close of a fight? Seems like you came back pretty quick."

Only then did I remember that I was still an active participant in the Bullet of Bullets tournament. I blinked and looked around, noticing that the previously bustling dome was only half-full now. Most of the first round was finished, with the losers being teleported back to the surface. My next opponent would be determined very soon, with the second round to follow.

But it was hard to imagine being able to fight anytime soon.

I looked first at Spiegel, who was shooting me a suspicious gaze from a slight distance, then back to Sinon, who stood right in front of me, then sighed lifelessly though slackened lips.

She put a dead-serious look on her face. "You're never going to make it to the final if that's how you're feeling after one fight. Get it together—I've got to collect what you owe me, remember."

She clenched a fist and pounded my shoulder again.

Without thinking, I grabbed her little hand with both of mine before it could be pulled away. I drew it toward my chest and put my forehead against it.

"Wh-wh…what are you doing?!" she yelped, trying to extract her hand, but I held fast.

Even the false warmth from that polygonal avatar's hand was more comforting than I could put into words. I felt the terrible chill of fear that had settled over my heart, and my body began trembling, well after the fact.

"…What's the matter…?"

As the seconds passed, I felt the resistance from that small, warm hand slowly ease away.

7

Sinon squinted, feeling a slight itch in her trigger finger.

She tried to rub the sensation loose against the side of her thumb, but the prickling feeling that plagued the core of her finger did not ease up. And she knew why.

It was Kirito. That rude, arrogant, insolent newcomer had squeezed her hand too hard.

Her common sense told her that this was impossible. Sinon was in the midst of a full dive through her AmuSphere, and no matter how hard anyone squeezed her hand, it could not possibly affect the flow of blood or the pressure on her nerves in real life. Every physical sensation she felt in this world was false, a machine-created signal sent directly to her brain via electronic pulses.

But...

The fact remained that Sinon still felt the pressure and warmth of the black-haired swordsman's grip. And that was two hours ago.

She gave up on trying to eliminate the sensation and put her hand back on the antimateriel rifle, secure on its stand. Her index finger traced the trigger, its springs set to light sensitivity. The grip of the Hecate II, which had accompanied her through countless battles, melted into her hand like an extension of her arm. Even then, the itching continued.

Sinon was crawling on her stomach beneath some bushes at the lip of a short cliff, waiting for her chance to snipe.

The map was "Crossroads of the Wilds": an intersection of two straight roads in the midst of parched highlands. The name of her opponent was Stinger. Roughly twelve minutes had passed since the start of their fifth-round battle, the first of the Block F semifinals.

If she won this, then no matter what happened in the final, she would gain entrance to the BoB battle royale tomorrow, Sunday night. But Stinger had won the same number of matches as she had—this would be no walk in the park.

Just because he shared a name with the portable Stinger missiles did not mean he had them at his disposal. His main weapon was the FN SCAR carbine rifle, which was quite dangerous on its own. With a high-functioning ACOG scope, the gun's bullet spray was much tighter and deadlier. If he could get within naked visibility range, Sinon wouldn't be able to stop him.

Fortunately for her, the two roads split the map into four quadrants, and it was impossible to pass from one to the other without traversing the center intersection. Since the two players started at least half the map away from each other, there was no way they could be placed in the same block.

So Stinger knew that he had to pass through the intersection in order to get Sinon within his SCAR's range, and she knew that she had to succeed at sniping him when he did.

Therefore, she expected that Stinger would delay his charge until the last possible moment, hoping to catch her when her concentration was exhausted. On the other hand, she couldn't deny the possibility that he would defy that expectation and charge early, so ultimately, her only choice was to keep staring through the scope, every nerve at full attention.

At the present moment, over half of the fifteen tournament blocks from A to O had finished their entire lineup of matches, and there were only about ten other battles currently in progress. Back in the dome and the first-floor hall, as well as pubs around the world, her match was being broadcast without interruption—and anyone watching Sinon vs. Stinger had to be bored out of their minds. Twelve minutes, and not a single shot had been fired yet.

On the other hand, the other Block F semifinal currently in progress had enough excitement to make up for the tedium of this one, with change to spare. That match featured a close-range specialist with two SMGs against an even closer-range fighter—one swinging a lightsword.

She couldn't lose concentration. But even still, Sinon couldn't help but think about the mysterious black-haired girl—er, boy.

When she finished her first-round fight in about ten minutes and returned to the waiting dome, Spiegel—Kyouji Shinkawa—greeted her with a rousing celebration. She thanked him briefly and returned to the original box seats, only to be surprised by Kirito beating her there. She hadn't expected him to win before she did, and she was striding over to offer a bracing compliment when she was hit with a different kind of shock.

Kirito, who had been so consistently impudent before the match, had his head in his knees and his hands around them, his downturned black head and slender shoulders trembling.

Poor thing. Fighting against a proper gun put that much fear in him, even after he won the match.

She reached out and patted the night camo jacket the boy was wearing.

Kirito jumped in surprise, and slowly, fearfully raised his head to look at her.

The pretty, delicate features that anyone would have assumed were feminine were painted with deep, terrible fear—like he had just peered over the abyss into Hell.

"...You look like you've seen a ghost," Sinon muttered. Kirito blinked several times in rapid succession and put on an awkward smile.

He muttered that he was all right, it was nothing, and Sinon asked him if the battle was really that bad. But the boy merely hid his face under that long black hair and sighed, offering nothing else.

She had no further obligation to be involved with him.

Kirito had intentionally utilized her misunderstanding about his avatar's gender to take advantage of her directions, shopping advice, and even followed her into the same changing room.

Of course, Sinon bore some fault for not requesting his name card and for assuming he was a girl. So more than half of her anger was really at herself for being careless.

After she'd been used like a tool by her classmates, Sinon swore she'd never rely on another person, she'd never need friends again. And yet she forgot that oath the instant the rare female *GGO* player asked her for simple directions.

It was fun, going shopping in the market and riding on the back of that three-wheeled buggy. She realized that she'd been smiling and laughing in *GGO* for the first time in ages. Sinon wasn't really angry that Kirito was a man. She was angry because she couldn't forgive herself for letting her defenses down around him.

Which was exactly why she was so pleased to see that Kirito won his first-round fight.

She needed to split that pretty face with a bullet from her Hecate to prove that she could be stronger than when she met him. And yet he had become a prisoner to his terror, a different person completely.

Before she realized what she was doing, Sinon hissed, "You're never going to make it to the final if that's how you're feeling after one fight. Get it together—I've got to collect what you owe me, remember."

She had clenched her fist and pounded his shoulder again.

But the next moment, his white hands clenched hers. He pulled it down to the breast of his fatigues.

"Wh-wh…what are you doing?!" she yelled, trying to pull away, but Kirito held her hand tightly, with a strength that didn't seem possible from his delicate body. His hands were cold as ice, and the breath that touched her skin was just as freezing.

At that point, an icon started blinking in Sinon's view, advising her to issue a harassment warning. If she touched the icon with her left hand or said the word, Kirito would be banished to Glocken's prison zone for a fair amount of time.

But Sinon couldn't move or speak.

She felt a strong sense of déjà vu from the sight of that fragile avatar trembling in fear and clutching her hand. She'd seen a girl suffering in this way before. It didn't take long before she realized that it was herself.

Not Sinon the sniper, but Shino Asada. Curled up in her bed, terrified of her memory of the scent of blood and gunpowder, whispering for someone, *anyone* to help.

The instant she recognized this, all the strength went out of Sinon's arm.

"...What's the matter...?"

He did not answer. But Sinon could feel it.

The black-haired character clinging to her hand—no, the nameless, faceless player behind the avatar—was plagued by the same darkness that Shino knew.

Sinon wanted to ask what happened. But just before the words could leave her mouth, his body was enveloped in pale light and disappeared. His next opponent had been determined, and he was whisked away to his second round battle.

She knew he couldn't put up a decent fight in that state. Sinon sighed.

The loser was returned not to the underground dome, but back to the hall of the regent's office. So if Kirito lost, she would likely not see him again today—if ever.

And that was fine. He wasn't a friend, just a person she ran across and accompanied to the office. She would forget his face and name by the day's end, and that was that.

Or so she told herself, as Sinon pulled her dangling hand back up to her chest.

And yet, Kirito defied her expectations and won the second-, third-, and now fourth-round fights with just his lightsword and handgun.

Just once, during the waiting period between her own fights, was Sinon able to catch a glimpse of Kirito on the monitor. His style was that of reckless suicide strikes, all desperate fury and ferocity. He shot back at the assault-rifle-toting AGI type with the Five-Seven handgun Sinon had picked out for him as he charged headlong, ignoring any bullets that hit his extremities and using that lightsword to block the fatal shots in a display of mad bravado. Once he'd closed the gap entirely, he sliced clean through the enemy and his rifle.

Not a single player had fought this way in either the first or second Bullet of Bullets. Sinon could only watch, wide-eyed, amid the murmuring surprise filling the dome.

At that rate, Kirito was quite capable of reaching the final of Block F. But how to fight someone with such an extreme style?

Even after her next match started, Sinon continued to mull over her strategy. At the same time, she couldn't help but wonder about Kirito the player.

That natural, curious smile when they were shopping for gear. The cool, aloof attitude once she learned that he was a man. The weakness he showed as he clung trembling to her. And now, the demonic savagery of the blue blade he used to slay his foes.

Which one was the real Kirito? And why couldn't she keep herself from thinking about him?

Plagued by irritation without a reason, Sinon bit her lip and kept her eye pressed to the high-power scope.

On the left side of the crossroads a kilometer away, a large shadow leaped out from the profile of the cliff. Sinon adjusted the Hecate's crosshairs automatically. The wind was coming at 2.5 meters from the left. Five percent humidity. She pulled the center of the glowing reticle just a bit above the shadow and tugged the trigger on the very first contraction of the bullet circle.

A blast.

Through the scope, she saw the .50-caliber bullet tear a tunnel of heat haze through the air. Its gentle spiral down and to the left connected with the upper half of the shadow.

"...Oops," she muttered, yanking the Hecate's bolt handle. The empty cartridge popped out and the next round fit into the chamber.

The shadow that crumbled away did not belong to her opponent Stinger, but a simple mass of stone about three feet across. The next instant, an even larger silhouette emerged from the same direction, spitting up dust.

It was a High-Mobility Multipurpose Wheeled Vehicle (HMMWV), better known as a Humvee. Vehicles were not the personal property of either player, but left somewhere in the map as a bonus awaiting whoever found it first. Sinon immediately noticed that despite the fact that the cars in the stage appeared in pristine condition, this one's front bumper was already dented. That meant he had rammed that first rock out into the open with it.

Stinger, sitting in the driver's seat, must have known that Sinon's weapon was a bolt-action rifle that couldn't fire consecutively. He also knew that she would be camping out, watching the intersection he needed to traverse.

Therefore, he set up a plan to use the Humvee to knock the boulder into the crossroads and cause her to fire, then race through the empty space before she could get off her second shot.

It was a good plan. In the space of time that Sinon pulled the handle, the car was already halfway through the intersection. She had time for one more shot, if that, and no time to focus on aiming.

But Sinon did not panic.

Although Stinger had stolen the sniper's best weapon—the first shot without a warning bullet line—he had given her valuable intel. The trajectory that her first shot traveled was now burned into her mind. If she kept her wits about her, the second would move the same way. If she made use of that information, she could fire with much greater precision on the second shot.

Sinon shifted the barrel and quietly pulled the trigger. Another blast.

The bullet honed in on the Humvee's small side window as if sucked into it, easily piercing the heavy bulletproof glass.

The next moment, the vehicle shot sideways, rolling up against the rocks at the shoulder of the road. It stuck against the far cliff, and dark, reddish smoke billowed out of the hood.

"If you'd jumped out of the car and run, you might have been able to avoid the bullet line," she admonished, loading her third bullet. With her eye still stuck to the scope, Sinon kept the burning Humvee in her reticle. Stinger did not appear for several seconds, which suggested that he might have died right in the driver's seat. She did not ease herself out of firing position.

Sinon crawled out of the bushes and got to her feet only after the *Congratulations!* message appeared in the sunset sky.

The match time was nineteen minutes and fifteen seconds. She had cleared the semifinals.

Now she had her ticket for tomorrow's BoB main event. But Sinon didn't even crack a smile, much less pump a fist. Her mind was already on the Block F final match coming up in moments.

She had no doubt that the mysterious newcomer Kirito had won his semifinal match in shorter time than she did. His opponent was a close-range fighter who held an SMG in either hand. No matter how many bullets you could produce, once the swordsman got within range, he would slice his foe with that fatal energy blade before you could carve his HP away. Kirito's reaction speed was so quick that he could predict the bullet prediction line. If you wanted to beat him in close combat, you needed one of those M134 miniguns.

So Sinon kept the Hecate secure in hands, frozen in place until the teleporter carried her to the next battle. A few seconds later, she was moved not to the domed waiting room, but the preparatory space before the final. As she expected, the name of her opponent displayed above the hex-panel floor was *Kirito*.

When she opened her eyes after the next teleportation, Sinon saw an elevated bridge, arrow-straight, and a bloodred sun in the process of setting.

It was the "Transcontinental Highway" stage. The size of the map was the same as the others before it, but there was no way to scale down the hundred-yard-wide highway that crossed the map from east to west, so it was actually quite a simple, narrow area to fight in.

On the other hand, with all the countless cars, trucks, downed helicopters, and bulging chunks of pavement, there was no way to see from one end to the other with the naked eye.

Sinon spun around and confirmed that she was on the eastern edge of the map. Which meant that Kirito, her opponent, was at least five hundred yards to the west.

She glanced at her surroundings and started running. Her target was the double-decker sightseeing bus ahead on the right. Sinon raced inside the ajar rear door and climbed the stairs to the second deck. She threw herself belly first onto the floor of the center aisle and deployed the bipod, pointing the gun straight ahead—out through the panoramic viewing window at the front of the bus. She was in firing position, the front and rear flip covers on the scope open.

The sun was directly ahead. That meant that no matter where she was hiding, there would always be the danger that the sunlight would catch the lens of her scope and tip the enemy off. There was no easier target than a sniper exposed.

But the mirror-coated windows of the bus would help hide the reflection of her scope. It was also tall enough that she could see over nearly all of the impediments below.

Kirito was probably making his way over at high speed, flitting from cover to cover. With his skills, there was no way she'd be able to snipe him with the bullet line visible; Sinon would only have one chance: while he was unaware of her location.

I can hit him. I know I can, she told herself, and pressed her right eye to the scope.

Even she couldn't fully explain what drove her to desire this victory so badly. Yes, she had helped him with directions and shopping advice while he was hiding his gender from her, and he had watched her change clothes.

But that was all that happened. She hadn't suffered any item or monetary loss, and the only underwear he'd seen belonged to her avatar. They'd spent less than an hour together from meeting on the streets of Glocken to separating in the domed auditorium. She could easily forget something that brief.

Yet Sinon wanted to beat Kirito with such a fiery passion that all the countless other battles she'd fought in *GGO* paled in comparison. Yes, even Behemoth, the terrible minigun user. Why was she so fixated on someone who'd just shown up here today, and who insisted on being a minority lightsword fighter rather than a gunner...?

...No.

No, maybe she already knew the reason why.

Because somewhere in my heart, I haven't fully accepted him as my enemy. When his frozen hands clutched mine as he trembled atop that hard, uncomfortable seat, an emotion without a name was born in my heart.

Sympathy? No.

Pity? No.

Empathy...? Definitely not.

I don't empathize with anyone. There is no human being alive who can bear the darkness that plagues me. I've had that hope and been betrayed before, over and over and over and over.

Only my own strength can save me now. I'm in this spot because I've learned that fact.

I don't want to know Kirito's problems, and I don't need to. One emotionless bullet will destroy his bewitching avatar and bury it among the countless other targets I've reduced to dust. Then I'll forget him.

That's all I need to do.

Sinon stared through the scope and traced the trigger with her finger.

Which was why, when she saw the black silhouette stand against the red of the setting sun, Sinon forgot her sniper's instincts for a moment and gasped.

"Wha...?"

Long black hair rippling in the breeze. Slender limbs in night-time fatigues. A lightsword handle hanging from his belt. It was Kirito.

But he wasn't running. He didn't even seem to care about hiding. He was walking, very leisurely, down the center of the highway on a slightly raised bulge in the road. It was a completely defenseless maneuver, absolutely unlike the last match.

Does he think that he can dodge my shot, even without the bullet line?

The challenge sparked her mind like an explosion. Sinon trained her scope's crosshairs right over Kirito's head. Just as she was about to put her finger to the trigger, she realized that her conjecture from a second ago was mistaken.

Kirito wasn't facing forward. His face was downcast, his body devoid of strength. He was simply moving his legs one after the other. It was a lifeless plodding, the polar opposite of his possessed charge in the clip she'd seen earlier.

He could not possibly dodge Sinon's shot in this state. The Hecate II fired bullets far faster than the speed of sound, so he wouldn't hear the gunshot until it was too late. With his face to the ground, he wouldn't even notice the flash of the muzzle.

Meaning...Kirito had no intention of dodging at all. He would take her shot and lose on purpose to bring an end to the match. After earning the right to appear in the final battle tomorrow, he didn't care about the battle with Sinon at all. That was all it meant.

"...Why...you..." she rasped.

She put her finger to the trigger again and tightened it. The green bullet circle appeared and rapidly pulsed over Kirito's head. Its frantic rate indicated the wild state of her heartbeat, but the wind was weak and the target was only four hundred yards away. If she fired, the shot would land.

Beneath her index finger, the trigger spring squeaked. But her finger relaxed again. She tensed it, and the spring squeaked. Then back.

"...Screw this!" she yelped, the wailing of a crying child.

At the same moment, Sinon squeezed the trigger. The roar of the .50-caliber rifle filled the tourist bus and the large front window cracked cloudy white and exploded outward.

The bullet split the crimson sunset sky and passed well over a foot away from Kirito's right cheek to slam into the belly of a car on its side far behind him. A pillar of fire erupted, followed by billowing black smoke.

Kirito stumbled a bit at the air pressure from the 12.7 mm bullet passing by his head, then stopped and looked up. The only readable thought on his feminine features was disbelief that she would miss. Sinon stared at that face through the scope, pulled the bolt handle, and fired a second round without missing a beat.

This one flew far over Kirito's head and disappeared into the far distance.

Reload. Pull trigger. The third shot gouged a huge hole into the asphalt to the left of his black boots. Reload. Fire. Reload. Fire. Reload, fire.

The sixth cartridge clattered next to Sinon briefly, then disappeared.

Through her scope, the unharmed Kirito continued to stare at her questioningly. Sinon got to her feet unsteadily, cradling the Hecate in her arms, and walked up the aisle of the bus. She made her way through the frame of the missing windshield and hopped down onto the street.

After a few dozen steps, when she was just fifteen feet away from Kirito, Sinon stopped. She stared down the unmoving swordsman dressed in black.

"...*Why?*"

Kirito understood the question and the accusation behind it. His black eyes wavered and returned to his feet. Eventually he spoke, but his voice was as bland and lifeless as an NPC's.

"...My goal is to appear in tomorrow's final—that's all. I have no reason to fight now."

She expected that answer, but couldn't stand to hear it. That disgust flooded her chest and pushed out her next sentiment.

"Then you should have taken that gun and shot yourself the moment the match started. Did you not want to waste the ammo? Or did you think that standing still so I could rack up one more on the kill counter would satisfy me?!"

She took another step toward the silent man.

"It's just a single match in a stupid VR game—you can think whatever you want! But don't force me to play along with your stupid philosophy!" she shouted, her voice shaking. Even she knew that she didn't really believe what she was saying.

If anything, Sinon was forcing him into her philosophy. If what he did was unacceptable, she should have hit him with the first shot and forgotten it ever happened. Instead, she wasted six shots trying to intimidate him, and now she was hurling all her emotions at him up close. If anyone was acting irrationally, it was her.

But...

She still couldn't stop herself. She couldn't stop the arms cradling the Hecate from trembling, the muscles of her face from scrunching up, or the teardrops that spilled over the rims of her eyelids.

The silhouette of Kirito against the setting sun across the horizon still had its eyes shut tight. His mouth was clamped down.

Eventually, the tension drained out of the delicate avatar, and he spoke in a weak voice with just a hint of emotion behind it.

"...I...I once blamed someone the same way you did, just now..."

"..."

Kirito glanced at Sinon and dipped his head briefly.

"...I'm sorry. I was wrong. It's just a game, just one match, but that's exactly why I need to do everything I can...Otherwise, I don't have a reason or the right to live in this world. I should know this already..."

The swordsman from abroad raised his head and stared into Sinon with those black eyes.

"Will you give me a chance to make it up to you, Sinon? Will you fight with me?"

In her surprise, she momentarily forgot her anger. "Right now...?"

The BoB prelims were more like encounters, battles that began without knowledge of the enemy's location. Now that they had come face-to-face without fighting, there was no way to return to the starting conditions.

But Kirito smiled weakly and pulled the Five-Seven from his waist holster. She tensed up automatically, but he held out a hand to stop her, and pulled the slide. The cartridge flew out and he caught it in midair, then returned the gun to the holster.

Twirling the 5.7 mm bullet in his fingers, Kirito said, "You've still got ammo, right?"

"...Yes. One shot."

"Let's have a duel, then. How about...we separate to ten yards. You use your rifle, I'll use my sword. I'll toss this bullet up, and the fight begins when it hits the ground. How's that?"

Sinon was less surprised by this than exasperated. She did not realize that her anger from moments ago had somehow dissipated away.

"Are you thinking that's going to make for a proper fight? There is no way I can miss at ten yards. Between my skill proficiency, my base stats, and my gun's specs, the game will *guarantee a bull's-eye.* You won't even have time to swing your lightsword. It would be the same thing as committing suicide."

"You don't know unless you try," Kirito sassed, his red lips curling into a grin.

The moment she saw that look, a buzz ran up Sinon's spine.

He was serious. The swordsman actually thought he could beat her in a serious, Old West–style duel.

Yes, there might only be one more bullet in the Hecate II's magazine, which made him feel that if he could somehow dodge that shot, he could win. But that was foolish. You couldn't "somehow" do anything to a bullet that was guaranteed to hit. The speed, accuracy, and power of her gun was miles ahead of that antique revolver in the shopping mall's bullet-dodging game.

But—what if there *was* something to Kirito? She couldn't help but want to see that.

Sinon nodded and said, "All right. That will settle this."

She turned around and took ten paces to the east along the center divider, then turned back to the sun.

They were exactly ten meters apart. She raised the Hecate, set the stock against her shoulder, and spread her feet to brace against the recoil.

In the real world, even the strongest man could not accurately fire an antimateriel sniper rifle from a standing position, but with enough strength in *GGO*, it was possible. The blowback would knock her off her feet, of course, but with only one bullet, that didn't matter.

She pulled the bolt and popped the last remaining bullet into the chamber.

With her cheek pressed to the receiver, Kirito's figure filled the entire scope, even at minimum zoom.

There was none of the lifeless emptiness in his girlish beauty anymore. His obsidian eyes sparkled and flashed, and a confident smile played across his lips.

With the bullet from the Five-Seven held between the fingers of his extended left hand, Kirito removed the lightsword from his waist. He flicked the switch on with a thumb, and the pale blue energy blade buzzed to life.

At this point, anyone watching the Block F final had to wonder what the hell these two were doing. But that wasn't their concern. One bullet against one blade. It shouldn't have been a proper fight, but the prickling tension that curled the hairs on the back of Sinon's neck was real.

There is something to him.

The Hecate's sights slipped just a little bit. On the other end of the scope, Kirito's lips moved.

"...Here goes, then."

He flicked his thumb. The bullet went spinning, spinning, high into the air, glittering in the evening sun like a ruby.

Kirito dropped into a crouch, his left side leaning forward and the lightsword in his right hand drooping downward. It was an easy stance, not a hint of tension from his toes to his fingertips. Yet there was an invisible pressure exuding from that fragile avatar, the pressure of one whose heart is in the sights of a gun.

Sinon could tell that her own senses were heightening as well. The 5.7 mm bullet spinning through the air was moving far too slow. All sound disappeared, leaving only her body and the Hecate II. In fact, even the boundary between those two things was gone. Shooter and gun became one, a precision machine designed to hit a target with a high-speed bullet.

The white reticle and green circle vanished from her view. The bullet dropped in slow motion, tumbling, turning, before the silent swordsman. It passed through the field of her scope and vanished, but she could still feel it: It spun end over end as it approached the pavement; its pointed head touched the asphalt; the game system determined that two objects had collided, generating the appropriate sound effect; the sound echoed through the AmuSphere as an electronic pulse, into the auditory center of Sinon's brain, and—

Ting.

The instant the sound hit her ears, she squeezed the trigger with her index finger.

Within her accelerated consciousness, Sinon witnessed and processed with vivid detail a number of phenomena that occurred in the next second.

Orange fire spat from the large muzzle of the Hecate.

Across the way, blue lightning split the darkness at a diagonal angle.

Two sparkling comet lights split left and right into the distance.

As the massive recoil of the antimateriel rifle toppled her backward, Sinon belatedly understood the meaning of what she'd seen.

He cut the bullet.

The instant that the bullet serving as the signal to duel hit the ground, Kirito sliced the lightsword diagonally, splitting the .50-caliber bullet that should have killed him in two. The two comet tails she saw were the pieces of the shattered bullet grazing the sides of his body as they flew apart.

But that was impossible!

It would be one thing if he guessed on the bullet's trajectory, swung in blind desperation, and got lucky. But Sinon had deliberately pointed away from the center of his avatar, aiming for his left leg instead.

Large-caliber bullets like the ones the Hecate shot added an extra effect called Impact Damage. At this ultraclose range, the impact effect meant that even a hit on the arm or leg would spread damage to the entire body, easily wiping out his HP.

Being brand-new to *GGO* and having zero knowledge about guns, Kirito could not possibly have understood this. So if he was going to guess the trajectory of the bullet, he would protect the center of his body, naturally.

Yet he accurately caught the bullet screaming toward his left thigh with the blade of his lightsword. It wasn't a gamble. At that range, that speed, without any bullet-line assistance. But why—*how*?

Even in that moment of shock, Sinon's arms kept moving. She took her left hand off the Hecate as she fell and tried to pull out the MP7 on instinct.

But before that could happen, Kirito closed the thirty feet that separated them with a lightning dash, bearing down on her. The blade in his right hand growled and lit her world blinding blue.

She was going down.

But Sinon did not shut her eyes against the blow. She kept them open, taking in the fan of sleek black hair splayed out against the giant setting sun—

And then everything stopped.

Sinon was still falling backward with the Hecate in one hand and the MP7 in the other, but still she did not hit the pavement. Kirito's left arm was around her back.

And in his right hand, the glowing blade was held still against her defenseless throat. The growling plasma sword and the distant whistle of the wind were the only sounds.

Kirito was crouching deep on his left knee, while Sinon lay flat on her back. It was like a still frame from a dance scene.

Those pitch-black eyes were right in front of her face. She'd never let anyone get this close in the virtual world, much less the real world, but Sinon didn't even think about this. She just stared back at him.

"...How did you predict where I'd shoot?"

His lips parted on the other side of the energy blade.

"I saw your eye through the lens of your scope."

Her eye. Her line of sight.

The black-haired swordsman was claiming that he could tell where the bullet was going based on her line of sight.

Sinon had never considered that someone in this virtual world might have that skill. A sensation, much like a chill but not entirely, shot through her back to the top of her head.

He was strong. Kirito's strength transcended this VR game.

But that made the question even more pertinent: Why had he been curled into a ball and trembling in the corner of that waiting-room dome? Why had he clung to Sinon's hand with those freezing fingers?

An even quieter question escaped her lips.

"If you have this much strength, what could possibly terrify you?"

Kirito's eyes wavered slightly, and after a brief silence, he sounded like he was holding something back.

"This isn't strength. It's just technique."

For a moment, Sinon forgot about the deadly blade of light pressed to her throat, and shook her head fiercely.

"Liar. You're lying. You can't cut a bullet from the Hecate with technique alone. You know something. How did you get that kind of strength? That's...that's what I'm here to learn..."

"Then let me ask you," he muttered, his voice low but burning with blue flame, "if that bullet could actually kill a player in real life—and if you didn't kill them, either you or someone you care about would die—could you still pull the trigger?"

"...!!"

Sinon forgot to breathe. Her eyes bulged.

For a second she wondered, *Does he know?* Did this mysterious visitor know about the event hidden in the darkness of her past, the incident that had blackened her life as she knew it?

No, he doesn't. He doesn't know. But he's probably experienced... something like it...

The hand supporting Sinon's back tensed hard, then relaxed. Kirito lifelessly shook his head, the tips of his long bangs brushing her forehead.

"...I can't do it anymore. That's why I'm not truly strong. I...I didn't even know the real names of the two or three people I cut down...I just shut my eyes, covered my ears, and tried to forget everything..."

Sinon didn't understand what he meant.

But one thing was for certain. Kirito harbored the same darkness and fear that dwelt within her. And in the time that he'd spent waiting for the next match in the dome, something had happened—something that drudged up the darkness he'd thought was buried.

The MP7 slipped out of Sinon's hand and clattered on the asphalt. Her empty hand rose upward on invisible strings to approach Kirito's white cheek, beyond his glowing sword.

But just before her fingertips could brush him—

The impudent smile returned to his face. There was still a look of pain in those dark eyes, but he shook his head and stopped her hand with a word.

"So…shall we assume that I've won the duel, then?"

"Huh…? Oh. Umm…"

She blinked in confusion, unable to switch gears. He leaned in even further.

"Would you mind resigning, then? I'd prefer not to slash a girl in two."

It was that shameless, rude, show-offy line that finally got Sinon to reassess the situation—pathetically and miserably immobile, held tight with a hand on her back and a sword at her throat, their bodies pressed together. And this scene was being broadcast live into the tournament dome, the regent's office, and every pub in Glocken.

Sensing the blood rushing to her cheeks, Sinon gritted her teeth and spat back, "I'm glad I get another chance to fight back. You'd better stick around in tomorrow's final until I have a chance to take you down myself."

Then she turned her face away and shouted the command to resign.

The time of battle was eighteen minutes and fifty-two seconds. Block F preliminaries for the third Bullet of Bullets were over.

(to be continued)

AFTERWORD

Hello, this is Reki Kawahara. Thank you for picking up *Sword Art Online 5: Phantom Bullet*, the fifth in this series and my tenth published book overall.

When it comes to online games, there are two other very popular genres aside from the MMORPG: the Real-Time Strategy (RTS) game, and the First-Person Shooter (FPS) game.

I enjoy both types, but if I get started on RTS games, I'll run out of paper, so let's put that aside for now.

As the name suggests, an FPS is a gun-based game in which the player sees directly from the perspective of the character he plays. This genre arose in America, and in terms of the number of games and players, they still easily lead the world. When playing online against them, I've often wondered if I was actually up against the great sniper Simo Häyhä. Just imagine me running around at top speed, then hearing a tiny *pop* from across the map, only to fall to the ground with blood streaming from my forehead. Or if it's a close-quarters fight, they'll easily dodge around my assault rifle fire, then run up and shank me with a knife (in this case, I wonder if they're actually Steven Seagal reborn). Of course, that could be my own lack of skill speaking!

PvP play in MMOs is very heavily affected by differences in level and gear, but FPSs are much more determined by player skill, as there's little difference between characters' in-game abilities. One of the inspirations for the Phantom Bullet arc in *SAO* was a desire to depict that kind of gaming "strength."

The problem is that while I enjoy FPSs, I know next to nothing about actual guns...You might think that I'm tossing out all kinds of gun names and terminology like it's second nature, but that's entirely an illusion I've put on. I'm sure that an actual expert in guns would read this and throw the book aside in disgust, but I hope you can accept any inaccuracies as "just within the game."

To my editor, Mr. Miki, for fixing up my drafts despite the many other tasks on his plate, to abec for the delightful illustrations of our two (*hah!*) heroines in this volume, and to you, dear reader, for noting my previous warning about getting off track last book and continuing onward anyway, I dedicate head shots of pure gratitude. Hope to see you next time!

Reki Kawahara — June 10th, 2010